The
HIGHWAYMAN
CAME WALTZING

A NOVELLA

OTHER BOOKS BY KATHLEEN BALDWIN

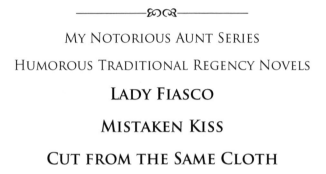

MY NOTORIOUS AUNT SERIES

HUMOROUS TRADITIONAL REGENCY NOVELS

LADY FIASCO

MISTAKEN KISS

CUT FROM THE SAME CLOTH

FROM TORTEEN (MACMILLAN)

EXCITING NEW REGENCY ROMANCE YA SERIES
THE STRANJE HOUSE NOVELS

A SCHOOL FOR UNUSUAL GIRLS

EXILE FOR DREAMERS

REFUGE FOR MASTERMINDS

CONTEMPORARY TEEN FANTASY

DIARY OF A TEENAGE FAIRY GODMOTHER

THE
HIGHWAYMAN
CAME WALTZING

A TRADITIONAL REGENCY ROMANCE

NOVELLA

FROM AWARD WINNING AUTHOR
KATHLEEN BALDWIN

INK LION BOOKS

Published by Ink Lion Books™

Baldwin, Kathleen (2015) The Highwayman Came Waltzing, a Novella
ED 050115

PRAISE FOR
THE HIGHWAYMAN CAME WALTZING:

———————ℰᴏᴄ℞———————

The following comments are from reviews of the original publication of this novella in an anthology. The Highwayman Came Waltzing has since been revised and reedited for your reading pleasure.

"...filled with romance and I found that time flew by at warp speed as I read." **– Huntress Reviews**

"These thieves are not what you expect...well-written and pleasurable romp through the regency period.
–ArmchairInterviews.com

"...true love is found on the dance floor."
– Romantic Times, *4 ½ Stars*
(referring to Waltz with a Rogue anthology in which The Highwayman Came Waltzing appeared as the lead novella.)

———————ℰᴏᴄ℞———————

Author's Note

This novella is a tribute to Alfred Noyes, inspired by his romantic poem, *The Highwayman*. You'll find several verses echoed in the chapter headings, and the complete poem is available at the end of the book.

This is an improbable tale written strictly for your delight and enjoyment. Should you happen to crave more information about the highly romanticized, sometimes brutal truths behind the real highwaymen of myth and legend, please visit my website at www.KathleenBaldwin.com.

Until then, take a deep breath; close your eyes to harsh realities, and stroll with me into fictional Claegburn Woods where we will enter the lives of a rather unusual band of Robinhoodlums.

Prologue
The Moon Was a Ghostly Galleon

1814, night in Claegburn Woods

"IF THE PRIZE IS BIG ENOUGH, this will be our last venture." *The Frenchman* donned a black mask and a plumed tricorn, tilting the three-cornered hat to a jaunty angle.

Bertie grumbled and climbed up into the birch tree. "If you expect me to be glad about that, *don't*. It'll be dull as old porridge without these little outings."

Little outings, indeed.

"You know perfectly well we have to stop." *The Frenchman* glanced pointedly at their two smaller companions in crime. One stood in the upper branches of a tree directly across from Bertie. The other one danced and twirled in a small clearing deeper in the woods. They were a merry group of highwaymen, but . . . "It's too great a risk for the twins."

A sound from the road sent *The Frenchman* scampering up into the tree beside Bertie. Four of them hid in Claegburn Woods that night. Three perched in the trees. The fourth thief, garbed in flowing gray, raised a flute to her lips and prepared to chill their victims' souls with images of ghosts and haunting melodies of the afterlife.

"We've luck on our side. The night is playing along," *The Frenchman* whispered, and climbed higher to have a better look. Mist floated through the woods, enough to hide them, but not so much that someone who knew this patch of forest couldn't find their way. Someone like the notorious Highwayman.

Perfect.

"Aye." Bertie gestured toward the road. "And here comes our pigeon, ripe for the plucking."

"I knew he couldn't resist the lure of a shortcut." *The Frenchman* nudged Bertie with a grin and called out a warning to the others, "Get ready!"

They crouched in the branches of gnarled beech trees, alert and ready to spring. Farther back in the glade their accomplice danced into position. As if joining in the game, the moon sailed behind clouds, darkening the misty woods, transforming it into a frightening haunt alive with undulating silver and black shadows.

They watched the lonely stretch of road that cut through Claegburn Wood as their quarry, a wealthy baron, traveled home from a sumptuous dinner and musical evening at Mulvern manor. The large black landau lumbered to a stop in front of a crooked signpost. Coach lamps flickered through the darkness, casting thin yellow rays on a tilted marker. The driver hesitated and leaned forward studying the signpost. Then, with a scratch of his head, he did as the sign directed and turned the cumbersome black vehicle down the fork in the road.

It bumped and wobbled toward those lying in wait. *The Frenchman*'s heart banged like a woodsman's axe. Tangled beeches and towering silver birch soon swallowed up the hapless coach; branches scraped against its sides and roof. The coach was nearly beneath them now. Bertie stifled a chuckle when the footman, hanging onto the rear guard, swore as he tried to dodge twigs and whipping branches. Passage slowed, until the vehicle came to a dead halt at a log fallen across the road.

The coachman stared glumly at the offending roadblock, but when the forlorn strains of a flute whispered through the trees, he clutched his whip, holding it high and upraised as if warding off whatever evil was about to befall him. The screech of an owl, or the yip of a fox, would not have startled a burly man such as this driver. But the faint, hauntingly beautiful flute never failed to make sturdy men quake.

The coachman gulped. His voice was hoarse and shaking. "Who g-goes there?"

The passenger door opened partway, impeded by branches. The footman jumped down, breaking off twigs, and shoving through the branches to assist his master.

"What's all this then?" The owner of the coach, a balding baron, tried to squeeze his plump belly through the door that would only open half way. "Why are we stopped?"

Neither of his servants answered.

"Is that music I hear?"

The moon crept out from behind swirling dark clouds. The coachman sucked in his breath. "Cor! Bless me! It's a ghost. There! In the trees." He pointed with his whip.

"Rubbish! There's no such thing as ghosts." The baron puffed himself up and slapped away branches making his way toward the front of the coach. "Where? It's so dark I can't see a blamed thing. Well, speak up, man. I don't have all night. Where's this ghost of yours?"

The Frenchman dropped with the lightness of an autumn leaf onto the ground, breathed feathery laughter into the pigeon's ear, and nudged the point of a short sword into the baron's chubby side. *The Frenchman* whispered the inevitable words, "Stand and deliver, *monsieur*."

"Ruddy hell!" The blowhard baron sputtered a string of foul curses and glanced sideways. No doubt, he hoped his servant would rush to his aid. But his footman's arms were already securely pinned, and good ole' Bertie had slipped a black hangman's hood over the quaking fellow's wigged head.

"We're dead men," the baron moaned.

The Frenchman responded with a husky accent. *"Non, monsieur.* Do exactly as you're told and you may yet live."

Mystical notes from the flute drifted through the darkness, gliding through the forest like a creature with ghostly talons, clawing the men's hearts with fear.

From a low-lying branch, the third bandit leapt catlike onto the roof of the coach, crept up behind the frozen coachman, and jabbed a pistol muzzle into his back. "Do not move. *Zis* is a very light trigger." In a trice, the highwayman covered the coachman's head with a black silk sack and tied his hands with a violet sash.

"I know who you are." The baron hissed, *"The Frenchman."* Prodded by the sword, he spun around. "Cursed scoundrel."

The Frenchman acknowledged the introduction with a mocking bow. *"Enchanté.* Now empty your pockets, Englishman. *Tout suite."*

The stodgy baron's thick eyebrows pinched together in a furious glower as he foraged through his pockets. At last, he produced a small leather bag. He held it aloft by the drawstrings before reluctantly dropping it into *The Frenchman's* outstretched hand.

"Tsk, tsk, *monsieur.* So few coins?" *The Frenchman* hefted the bag, jingled its contents, and flashed a wide grin. "Clever fellow. Now hand over *ze* other purse."

"What other purse?"

"*Le bon ruse.* You play the pauper." *The Frenchman* shrugged. "*C'est la vie.* Remove your clothes. I will take them and search later."

The baron's wife sobbed from the coach. "For pity's sake, Godfrey, give them what they want."

"French rabble." Godfrey balled his fists at his sides. "I'll see you hang for this."

With lightning speed, the masked bandit whipped a short sword across the baron's chest and popped off three vest buttons. "*Possiblé.* But first I will see your purse." The sword point moved to the next button.

"Stop! Those are pearl buttons."

"Ah! So they are." *The Frenchman* chuckled and, in one quick motion, sliced the rest of them from their moorings, caught them, and deposited the pearls in the deep pockets of a black greatcoat.

The baron muttered a volley of ear-scorching expletives. With his vest dangling open and *The Cursed Frenchman's* sword aimed at his gullet, he dug out a second bag of money.

"*Merci.*" *The Frenchman* pocketed the second purse.

The third thief jumped nimbly down from the top of the coach and pointed an antiquated flintlock pistol at their quarry. "I'll guard this fat one while you get *ze* jewels."

Bertie, who was busy tying the footman to the rear wheel,

growled at the smaller thief. "Hush!"

The baron's wife cowered inside the coach, bawling like a small child.

"*Pardon moi, madame.*" *The Frenchman* swooped off the black tricorn with its purple ostrich feather and bowed lavishly to the baroness who looked to be half her husband's age. The old rascal had done well for himself. "I must relieve you of *zis* stunning necklace." The needle sharp sword tip lifted the diamond collar from the lady's neck without making a scratch.

Still quivering, the baroness obediently reached back and unclasped the necklace, dropping it into *The Frenchman*'s gloved palm. Tears trickled down her cheek.

"*Non.* You must not cry, *madame.* Without these distracting diamonds, your beauty will captivate the gentlemen. Your husband, he will have to hire a battalion to protect you from all *ze* lovesick swains, *n'est pas?*"

The lady's tears abated instantly. She brought a hand to her breast where the jewels had hung and she blinked quizzically at the masked *Frenchman*.

"And now, *ze* ring, also, *se il vous plaît.*"

The baroness shook her head and leaned away, clutching her hands together. "No, not that. Please, I beg you. This ring belonged to my mother. It's all I have left of her. Please don't take it from me."

"Your mother?" *The Frenchman* pulled back.

The lady nodded.

"*Très bien.* Keep your mama's ring. I bid you, *adieu.*" *The Frenchman* bowed again, donned the tricorn with a flourish, and turned from the coach doorway to see the baron and the smallest thief scuffling.

A shot blasted to shreds the lyrical quality of the night.

A scream.

The horses skittered and snorted, jangling their harnesses. Godfrey's wife added her shrieks to the cacophony. The baron's baldhead glistened in the moonlight. He held a smoking pistol in his hand. The small bandit lay on the ground in front of him.

Motionless.

From the shadows, Bertie's club descended on Godfrey's head. The blow dropped him to his knees, and he toppled forward face down in the leaves.

The Frenchman ran to their fallen comrade, frantically checked for blood, and murmured a desperate plea – the French accent forgotten. "Dear God, please. Not our Bonnie." Finding no blood, *The Frenchman* struggled to hoist the unconscious bandit and drag her into the woods. "Help me."

Bertie grunted, jammed the club back in its sheath, foraged through the leaves to collect the fallen highwayman's flintlock and stuffed it into a pocket, then ran to shoulder the other side of the limp body.

Moonlight scarcely penetrated the thick canopy of beech

trees. Yet, even in the darkness, the highwaymen ran as if they knew the way by heart. Ahead of them, in the shadows of the glade, stood a dilapidated wooden cart hitched to a tired old pony.

A young woman draped in flowing silver-gray, who might easily be mistaken for a ghost, ran to them. "I heard a shot. What happened?" She reached for her twin. "Bonnie?"

The Frenchman had no time to soothe fears. "We must hurry."

As lithe as the curling fog around them, the ghost-like young lady climbed on the aged pony's back. *The Frenchman* took up the reins and clucked at the old farm horse to trot. Bertie sat on the rear seat, cradling the moaning bandit.

As the cart rolled ponderously down the rutted path, the young flute player leaned forward to stroke the aged pony's neck and begged the animal to hurry. The mare snorted, lifted her tired feet higher, and soon the cart was bouncing rapidly toward the dower house.

Chapter 1
She Whistled a Tune in the Window

Two days later.

Elizabeth sat curled up in the window seat of the upstairs parlor, going over figures in the account book, basking in the relative peace of the afternoon. Her Aunt Bertie sat nearby in her favorite chair, reading the newspaper and humming softly, and her grandmother stitched quietly.

Bonnie charged into the room, swinging her protective vest in one hand and wielding a small hammer in the other. She stopped directly in front of Elizabeth. "If I leave the lead ball lodged in the wood, it will make the vest that much stronger."

It was a question, of course, but Bonnie preferred to make challenging statements rather than beg for an answer. Elizabeth glanced up from her accounting. "If the wood is compromised, you ought to replace the slat as well."

"Oh bother." Bonnie stamped her foot and turned away to plop down on a small stool beside the hearth.

"Altogether too much work. I'll simply patch it. Besides, what are the chances of getting shot in the same place twice?"

"Don't say such things!" Aunt Lavinnia, Bonnie's mother, stood in the doorway, her hand over her heart. "I should hope you will never get shot again. *Anywhere.*"

"No, Mama, of course not." Bonnie set to work nailing down a new piece of tin over her punctured one.

"Good. Now, do exactly as Lizzy says. That contraption saved your life." Lavinnia positioned herself on the settee and pulled out a pile of sewing.

Bonnie muttered softly and continued doing a patch job instead of a replacement.

Elizabeth shook her head. Her cousin Bonnie had a stubborn streak inherited from their grandmother.

Bonnie's twin sister, Blythe, floated in behind her mother and sat down at the pianoforte. She toyed with nine notes, playing them over and over, rearranging and regrouping them into various melodies, while her twin's hammer tapped incongruously to the harmony.

Aunt Bertie rustled her newspaper and hummed all the louder.

Elizabeth marveled that they could all concentrate regardless of one another's activity. Despite the discordant racket in the parlor, she heard a noise outside in the yard and lifted the edge of the lace curtain. Lord Mulvern's coach rolled to a stop. She took a deep breath, set her book down on the table, and hurried across the worn Aubusson rug to her grandmother's chair.

Nana Rose's old straight-backed chair creaked when Elizabeth squatted down and grabbed hold of the arm. "Nana, Lord Mulvern is here. Promise you will be on your best behavior."

Her grandmother stiffened her spine and looked down her nose at Elizabeth. "What can you be saying, Lizzy? I am *always* on my best behavior."

"You know precisely what I mean. Try not to goad him."

"I will speak as I please to the man who murdered my sons and took away my—"

It was an old refrain. One they all knew by heart. "Not today, Nana. Please."

"Why should today be any different? He's still a murderer." Nana Rose nearly spit the words, belying her dignified appearance—starched black bombazine and cloud-white hair coiled up high enough to suit even Marie Antoinette. "Just as Cain slew Able and was punished, so—"

"Yes, of course. But I ask you, please consider the effect one slip of the tongue might have on your granddaughters. We cannot risk it." She patted her grandmother's hand and stood up to survey the rest of their family.

Blythe stopped playing the pianoforte, her face paler than usual.

"My dear." Elizabeth shook her head. "You mustn't worry. All will be well. Why don't you keep playing? It relaxes you."

"Yes, widgeon. Don't fret." Bonnie hopped up from her stool, tucked her chest protector into the bottom of the cupboard, and kissed her twin sister on the head. "It'll be a jolly bit of fun to see what he knows."

Blythe did not turn back to the piano keys. Instead, she lowered her eyes and folded her hands in her lap. Her flaxen hair fell forward, a silken curtain behind which she would hide.

Bertie dropped her newspaper to the floor and went to check on the arrival for herself. She stood boldly before the window, as a man might, without the slightest concern for propriety. She drew back the curtains with one hand, while rapping the knuckles of her other impatiently against the wall. "Blast. Double blast. What in blazes is Mulvern doing here?"

Nana Rose sniffed. "Probably got wind of something, the old goat." She didn't look up from the pile of black silk she was stitching. It was hard to distinguish which was the new fabric being sewn and which was her flowing black mourning dress.

"Lizzy is right. We must all mind our manners." Lavinnia glanced about the room genially, her frilly white mobcap bobbing cheerfully over her yellow curls. "Bound to visit, isn't he? He's family, after all. A gentlemanly thing to do." She surveyed her twin daughters. "Best foot forward, girls. Do try to smile, Blythe dear."

"Well, I don't like it." Bertie plunked back down into her chair, which hailed from King Henry the 8th's reign, and rubbed at the carved claw on the end of the arm. The wood had long ago lost its varnish. "Not a bit of it."

Elizabeth stood in the middle of the room. "We must all stay calm." She adjusted her serviceable brown muslin, hoping to hide the patchwork in the folds of the skirt, and pinched her cheeks. She considered her high cheekbones her only admirable asset. Pinching them was her last remaining bow to vanity.

Footsteps clattered in the entryway, and Lord Mulvern's booming voice echoed up the stairs as he groused at the housemaid. "No need to announce me, girl. Confound it. It's my house after all."

They all listened as their maid stoically insisted on protocol. "That's as may be, m'lord. But the ladies might require a moment to prepare for visitors." The spry housemaid scampered up the stairs ahead of him and dashed into the parlor. "It's his lordship, mum. And he's brought Master Trace with him."

"Trace? Here?" Elizabeth dropped down on the settee, astonished.

The gentlemen were not long behind. Lord Mulvern's

massive height took up most of the doorway. "You see what I must put up with." Removing his hat, exposing a head of frizzled graying hair, he addressed, not them, but his companion. "Confounded dower house. Packed to the gills with females. Can't take a step without tripping over a petticoat or something of the kind."

Nana Rose elevated her nose higher into the air. "Pray, do forgive us, your lordship. We will endeavor to go without undergarments if you insist. Indeed, on our current allowance, I'm surprised there's more than one petticoat to be found in the entire house."

Lord Mulvern frowned at his sister-in-law.

Elizabeth stood up and beckoned to him. "Come in, Lord Mulvern. Please be seated." She strained to see past his shoulders to catch a glimpse of Trace. "The maid said your stepson is with you?"

"So he is." Lord Mulvern thumped into the room and took possession of Elizabeth's seat on the settee next to Lavinnia. "With Napoleon tucked away for good this time, Trace's work is done. Sold off his commission. He's come home to hunt down the band of thieves terrorizing our neighborhood."

Elizabeth forgot to breathe as Trace entered the room. The friend she remembered had changed. There was nothing of the boy left in him. His face no longer held the smooth fullness of youth. Well-defined angles had taken its place. The small parlor filled with the clean scent of his shaving soap and the crisp smell of freshly pressed linen. His bearing was that of an officer in command: robust, regal. She stepped back. Indeed, the self-assurance in his blue eyes made her feel nervous and fascinated at the same time.

"Trace." Her voice scratched out, scarcely rising above a whisper.

"Lizzy?" He removed his hat, surveying her curiously. "I hope we find you well?"

She nodded, surprised to see his honey brown hair still curling intriguingly around his ears and neck. That, at least, had not changed.

Suddenly, Elizabeth wished she had not drawn her hair back so severely that morning. The single black knot at her neck could not possibly flatter her. She looked down at the ugly brown muslin gown. Oh, why hadn't she worn her other dress? She must look a ghastly old crow.

But what did it matter? What were such foolish thoughts to anything? She was an ape leader, at five and twenty, on the shelf for so many years she had grown moldy. Lord Mulvern's stepson would have no interest in an aging spinster. She smiled with all the dignity she could muster and offered him her hand.

Trace grasped it warmly. "A pleasure to see you again." He said it as if the sentiment almost surprised him.

She swallowed. "Yes. Welcome home." She nervously pulled her hand from his. There were no remaining seats, except the wobbly old spindle-legged chair against the wall. She glanced dubiously at it.

He followed her gaze and without hesitation moved the frail chair forward. "This will serve."

Elizabeth squeezed onto the end of the settee, forcing her Aunt Lavinnia to scoot closer to Lord Mulvern, and folded her hands in her lap. "We've read and reread all the accounts in the papers of your . . ." She faltered, searching for the right words.

Bertie nodded. "Heroism. Well done, lad."

"Yes." Nana Rose cleared her throat, sitting as stiff as if her back was strapped to a posture board. "Of course, we might've known of your stepson's accomplishments much sooner were our papers not a month old and missing pages." She glared at Lord Mulvern.

"Twaddle." Lord Mulvern snapped his fingers. "No sense wasting money on a second subscription. Tut, tut. It's enough I have 'em bundled up and sent over. A simple economy." He adjusted his brocade vest. "As usual, Rose, you've veered from the point. Trace has come home to hunt down our band of French cutthroats."

Lavinnia tilted her head sideways, a hand on her pink cheek. "Oh, but Adrian, they haven't cut any throats! Have they?"

Lord Mulvern leaned over and patted her hand. "No, my dear. A figure of speech. But, I daresay, the blackguards nearly killed Sir Godfrey two nights past."

Bertie turned sharply, suddenly very attentive. "What do you mean, *nearly killed him*?"

"Oh dear." Lavinnia held both hands to her face now. "Will the poor man recover?"

"Yes. Yes. Not to worry. He's fine. Nothing to it, save a lump the size of Mount Vesuvius on the back of his head. The good news is ole Godfrey shot one of the brigands—dead."

"Dead?" Bonnie nearly tipped over on her three-legged stool as she leaned forward, her eyes wide with interest. "Did you find a body? Were there great pools of blood in the road?"

"Bonnie!" Elizabeth called her reckless cousin to task.

Lord Mulvern harrumphed. "Quite right. Ought not discuss such gruesome things in mixed company."

Elizabeth shot Bonnie a warning glance.

Lord Mulvern continued with his subject. "Point is, we can't have these confounded thieves terrorizing m'neighborhood. Trace will get to the bottom of it."

"Hardly *terrorizing* the neighborhood." Bertie interjected.

"Doing a jolly good job of frightening my guests. Hanging sacks pulled over their heads. Guns. Swords. Enough to scare the life out of 'em, I can tell you that." Mulvern frowned at Bertie.

"What were the sacks made of, do you know?" Nana Rose actually sounded pleasant for once.

Lord Mulvern shrugged. "No idea. Black cloth of some

CUT FROM THE SAME CLOTH

sort."

"Ah, well, if you don't need them, we could put the cloth to use. Nothing goes to waste in this house. Perhaps you would send them over with the newspapers next time."

Bertie nearly choked. She glanced furtively at Elizabeth and cleared her throat. "What I meant to say is, none of the neighbors appear to be afraid."

"I see your point." Mulvern rubbed his jaw. "Somebody had to see something. Fact of the matter is they're all deuced tight-lipped. I've heard rumors though. Not only that, but this morning, I witnessed with my own eyes farmer Turner laying on new thatch. I'll wager that French rascal left him one of those famous bags of coins I've heard the servants whispering about."

"How lovely!" Lavinnia sighed happily and held up a piece of velvet cloth she was working on. "Mrs. Turner is about to have another wee one. New thatch will keep them warmer and dryer next winter." She smiled her approval on the group.

Lord Mulvern looked outraged at her suggestion. "Ain't lovely, Lavinnia. It's thievery! It's Sir Godfrey's money. Not theirs."

Lavinnia dropped her sewing into her lap and lowered her head. "Of course, you're right, my lord. I only meant it would be such a benefit for Mrs. Turner and their children."

He calmed down and moderated his tone. "Of course, Turner won't say how he got the coin. But it had to be one of those confounded velvet bags."

Nana Rose clucked her tongue. "Ought to have been *your coin,* Adrian, thatching that roof. He's your tenant. Their youngest almost died from the cold last winter. Unless, perhaps, you think you can stand the weight of another death on your soul."

"Don't start with me, Rose." Lord Mulvern flexed his jaw. "Look about you. This is practically a widows' and orphans' home I'm funding here. I'm spending every spare penny I have to take care of your lot. Although why I stand the expense is more than I can fathom. It isn't enough I'm bankrolling every poor relation in my brother's family, but you must go and give refuge to every destitute female for miles around."

"You're the soul of generosity, and we're exceedingly grateful." Lavinnia smiled admiringly at him. "You have a good heart."

Nana Rose coughed forcefully and grumbled under her breath. "A guilty heart. If you think the pittance you give us is going to stave off roasting in hell for your crimes, you best think again—"

"Would you care for some refreshments, Lord Mulvern? Trace?" Elizabeth quickly got up, grabbed the bell from her grandmother's side table, and rang it perhaps a little louder than necessary.

The maid appeared in the doorway.

"Food and drink, Maggie, for the gentlemen."

The maid whispered to Elizabeth, but in the silence, surely everyone overheard. "What would you have me bring, miss? The biscuits is gone. And we used the last of—"

"Surely, you and Cook can think of something." Elizabeth sat back down and attempted to take the reins of the conversation firmly in hand. She turned to Trace. "How do you plan to capture these highwaymen?"

"Our first—"

Mulvern interrupted. "That's why we've come. The tenants are as closemouthed as a passel of black-robed monks. I want the truth from you. Have those scoundrels left you money?"

"Money?" Elizabeth averted her eyes.

"Don't play coy with me, my girl. Fabric doesn't come cheap." He picked up a corner of the velvet lying in Lavinnia's lap. "Yet, here you are, sewing."

"You don't see me sewing." Bertie thrummed her fingernails against the wooden arm of her chair.

Mulvern ignored her. "Speak up, Lizzy. Did you receive money from the thieves?"

She opened her palm. The appropriate answer eluded her like a butterfly. "It's possible." She glanced at Trace. He sat on the rickety chair, alert, studying her, assessing the room. Altogether too observant.

She capitulated quickly, the lie souring her mouth, but there was no help for it. "Very well. Yes. We received a few coins. A small bag left on the porch. Enough for some fabric, but that is all. It could have been from anyone. Perhaps someone in the village felt charitable. As you said, many girls come here with nowhere to go—"

Mulvern slapped his hands on the frayed settee, flecks of aged horsehair puffed up around his fingers. "Betrayed by my own kin! You see?" He waved his hand through the air, indicting the inhabitants of the dower house, serving up his plight to Trace. "Even *they* are in collusion with the robbers."

The corner of Trace's mouth curved upward. "Clever, our highwaymen. Very clever. They ingratiate themselves with the whole neighborhood, thus protecting any information that may lead to their capture."

"Aye, and what are we to do about it?"

Trace rubbed his jaw thoughtfully. "I suggest, my lord, that you set a snare. Hold a ball. Order cakes and pastries from the village, just as you normally would for one of your dinner parties. Buy meats from the butcher. Cut flowers. Hire local musicians."

"A ball! Deuced expensive. And for what? So my guests may be waylaid by *The Frenchman* afterward. I think not." Mulvern crossed his arms stubbornly. "I shall simply stop entertaining at all."

Lizzy admired the eager gleam in Trace's eyes. A man ready for the hunt. He would be a formidable opponent.

"Ah, but that's the beauty of it." He leaned forward,

advancing his idea, pausing until he held everyone's attention captive. "You will not invite any guests. A *false* ball, if you will, to lure out our French rascal. The rogue is bound to hear of all the preparations. Such a night would be more temptation than he and his band can resist."

Lord Mulvern scratched at his wiry side-whiskers as he considered.

Elizabeth could not resist tampering with Trace's scheme. She tilted her head sideways. "Ah, I see. You intend to lay a trap. Perhaps a coach filled with men, guns primed and at the ready?"

Trace smiled approvingly. "Always the quick mind, Lizzy. Yes. That's it, exactly."

She tapped a finger against her cheek. "It's a pity to waste all that food for no guests. Not to mention the cost of musicians." She poised on the edge of the settee. "What if your French highwayman should peek into Lord Mulvern's windows? Will he not smell out the ruse?"

Mulvern grunted. "Let him. I'll post men to keep watch on the grounds. Blow the fellow into the next realm if he steps foot on m'place."

"Oh." She nodded, and then sighed heavily. "Unfortunately, you might accidentally shoot one of the children from the village merely coming to spy on your wonderful ball. You know how they love to see the adults dancing and dressed in their finery."

Nana Rose sniffed. "What's one more death to his credit, among so many?"

Lord Mulvern exhaled loudly and frowned at his former sister-in-law.

Lavinnia mewed. "I can understand the children's curiosity." Her round little shoulders lifted eagerly. "I would like to peek at it myself. A ball would be perfectly splendid. I haven't been to a ball this age. I know the twins would adore it."

Mulvern shifted uneasily.

Elizabeth could scarcely keep from smiling.

Trace sat, arms folded, with an all-too-observant look on his face again.

Time to bring the game to a close, Elizabeth decided. "Perhaps it would aid your ruse if we filled out the guest list? There are quite a number of us. We might lend credence to the appearance of a ball."

"Oh yes!" Bonnie jumped up, toppling the stool. "How wonderful it would be to eat cakes and meat. Any meat, aside from rabbit. Do you think you'll serve roast beef, Uncle Adrian? Oh, that would be heavenly."

Lord Mulvern sank back, somewhat colored in his cheeks. "Yes. Fine. We'll make it a family affair, eh?"

"How lovely." Lavinnia's pleasure shifted to alarm. "Oh, but what will we wear? The girls have nothing at all."

Lord Mulvern ran a finger around his collar. "It's a *false* ball. No sense fussing overmuch with your appearance."

Trace grinned sideways at Elizabeth. "It might perfect the illusion if the ladies were dressed properly. I believe, my lord, you still have a closet full of my mother's dresses, do you not? Perhaps the ladies might make over some of those to suit the occasion?"

Lord Mulvern looked down, a blanket of sadness thrown over his features. He mumbled and shook his head. "Dora's gowns? I don't know, I . . . they were . . . hers."

Nana Rose looked at Elizabeth. Elizabeth glanced covertly at Lavinnia. The three of them knew from personal experience the anguish underneath Lord Mulvern's hesitancy.

Lavinnia covered his hand with hers. "Never you mind, Adrian. We'll make do. You keep your dear departed wife's dresses just as they were."

"No." Mulvern sighed. "No, you're right. I suppose it would be better to put them to good use. I'll send over the gowns. Should have done so long ago."

Nana Rose tilted her head and squinted at him, curiously.

The maid interrupted, setting a teapot and two chipped cups and saucers down by the accounting book on the table. Elizabeth slipped the book away, tucking it under the settee. She lifted the teapot lid and grimaced. It was half-full of weak tea. She poured, setting a cup before each gentleman.

Trace thanked her graciously and managed to balance on the rickety chair and drink the pitiful concoction as if perfectly at ease.

Lord Mulvern took one look at the liquid in his cup and set the cup back on the saucer. "We must be going. I want to interview more of the tenants. I mean to discover exactly who's been receiving booty from these thieves."

Bertie snorted. "Won't say a word with you there, now will they?"

"Bertie is right." Trace set his cup down. "A fruitless venture."

Elizabeth spoke, quietly, uncertain of the wisdom behind her offer. "I'm to deliver sick-baskets for the vicar tomorrow. Perhaps I might ask if anyone has seen anything, and then report back to you."

Lord Mulvern brightened. "She's onto something there."

Trace agreed and asked if he might accompany her.

Mulvern's interest heightened. "Aye, and have a look about while Lizzy is talking to them. Bound to be a clue of some sort. Someone must've helped the wounded fellow. Godfrey said the blighter shrieked like a banshee. Had to have been shot well and good."

Bonnie clapped her hands together. "Perhaps they buried the bandit in the woods. Maybe you should search for a fresh grave."

Mulvern frowned at Bonnie. "Morbid speculation for a gel."

Lizzy hurried to cover her cousin's faux pas. "We've been lax in her choice of books—too many gothic novels, I'm afraid."

Mulvern tapped his fingers on his thighs. "On the other hand, she might be on to something. I ought to have some men comb the woods."

Elizabeth glared at Bonnie.

The minx waggled her shoulders back and forth, like a smug child who knows a secret. "I don't know what good it will do. Rained yesterday. A grave would be washed out. Wolves would have ripped apart the carcass and chewed the bones to pieces."

Mulvern grimaced. "Egad, child. How ghoulish! Yes, by all means, you must restrict her reading." He sniffed and straightened the lace at his cuff. "Aside from that, there haven't been wolves in that forest for a hundred years."

Bonnie shrugged. "Even if wolves didn't eat it, other scavengers would."

Blythe sat silently in the background, hiding behind her silken hair.

Elizabeth decided there had been enough precarious discussions for one afternoon. "Blythe, dear, will you play something for us?"

Without answering, Blythe turned to the pianoforte, her fingers moving over the keyboard with clarity and passion. In some passages, she played the keys so softly the hammers barely struck the strings, and at other times, with such ferocity that the old pianoforte fairly thundered.

Everyone listened, barely breathing, as she filled their minds with exotic cadences and images of midnight dancing among the trees of Claegburn Wood. The sewing lay forgotten in their laps and even restless Bertie did not move until Blythe struck the last note.

The room lay still, except for the ticking of the old clock on the cupboard. Trace inhaled deeply and glanced at Elizabeth, his brows raised. "She's talented." He leaned forward addressing Blythe. "That was beautiful. Enchanting. Was it a sonata perhaps? What is the name of the piece?"

She startled everyone by looking up, her pale blue eyes boring directly into his. "I call it, *The Highwayman's Rhapsody.*"

Trace recoiled, resting against the back of the decrepit chair, his brows pinched together. Calculating. Elizabeth panicked. She remembered from their youth that intense look in his eyes. She saw his mind leaping to solve the puzzle. He was far too quick to be toyed with in this manner. They were all foolishly underestimating him.

She sprang up, thanking the gentlemen for their visit.

Unhurriedly, Trace rose, hat in hand, brushing away some invisible lint from the crown. He stood beside her shoulder, suddenly inscrutable, and quietly quizzed her. "Tell me Lizzy, do you still play chess?"

She looked up, surprised that he'd remembered. "Not since our last game."

"Ah, then we must have a rematch. I can't recall who won the last time."

"Gudgeon. You know full well, I did."

The corner of his mouth curved up speculatively. "Did you? I could have sworn it was I."

Chapter 2

He Loved The Landlord's Daughter

BONNIE SQUEALED with delight when she saw the gowns Trace brought with him.

Elizabeth frowned at her young cousin's exuberance, but there was no repressing Bonnie.

The girl whirled around with a lovely pink silk dress hugged to her chest. "Oh, look, Lizzy! Is it not the most beautiful thing you have ever seen?" An instant later, her joy transferred to a pale blue damask, which she held up to Blythe. "This one is perfect for you." She dragged her sister to the mirror in the hallway and demanded her twin concede the statement.

Elizabeth touched Trace's arm. "Thank you for bringing the gowns so quickly. They could talk of nothing else last night."

"You'll need to alter them quickly. Lord Mulvern plans to

hold the ball as soon as possible. He has already sent to London for musicians. Oh, that reminds me." He pulled a small note from his chest pocket. "He sent this. For Lavinnia. An invitation, I believe, to help him decide upon the menu."

Elizabeth arched her brow in mock awe. "An invitation to the manor. I daresay Aunt Lavinnia will be in alt. We will have to pull her down from the ceiling."

"He means well, Lizzy. Always did far better by me than duty required. He's just preoccupied sometimes. Ever since mother—"

"I didn't mean . . ." She laid the note by the clock.

"I know." Trace turned to the stack of remaining dresses. "Which of these will you choose?" He lifted the edge of one of the gowns, briefly caressing the soft silk between his thumb and forefinger. "I thought this gold, against your dark hair. But, I see, you look very well in purple."

"Thank you." Elizabeth glanced down at her best dress, a plain, violet mourning gown. She had covered the worn hem with a darker purple ruffle and put a bow of the same color on each of the sleeves. This morning, she'd fiddled for far too long with her stubborn hair, trying to pin it up in loose curls. It probably looked more like a jumble of flapping crow's wings than anything else.

Foolishness.

She returned the conversation back to the business at hand. "The vicar only sent two baskets today. Shall we be on our way?"

The day was fine and clear, birds twittered happily, and only a few white clouds dawdled in the blue sky. Trace helped Elizabeth step up into Lord Mulvern's dogcart, pulled by a beast far superior to the ladies' tired old nag.

"This will be a rare treat. Daffodil, our mare, only trots under threat of death. Poor old thing."

Trace settled himself beside her. She could not help but breathe in deeply, savoring his shaving soap, the starched freshly pressed linen of his cravat, and a dozen other tantalizing scents that were uncommon in a house full of women.

He flicked the reins and the cart rolled briskly away from the dower house. "How bad is it?" he asked.

The question startled her. "What? How bad is what?"

"I'm not blind, Lizzy. You must tell me. How far has Mulvern's parsimony stretched? I will speak to my stepfather. Do you have enough to eat?"

Her hand lifted as if she were going to make a point and then dropped into her lap. "We get along well enough."

"Oh yes. So I see. Marvelous tea yesterday. Not everyone can afford such lavish—"

"Yes, well, it is not entirely his fault. He and Nana Rose are forever carping at one another. You may have forgotten."

"Ah, let me see if I recall." He pinched his mouth into the exact prune shape Nana Rose liked to use. "Not since Cain slew Abel, and Joseph's brothers threw him down the well, has a brother behaved so brutally. . ."

She laughed. "You do remember."

He steered adroitly around a puddle of rainwater. "Of course, I remember. It is you who are forgetful."

She sensed he was setting a trap. A gentle breeze blew pleasantly against her face before she answered. "I? What have I forgotten?"

"Promises."

Her stomach twisted uncomfortably.

An officer used to commanding his men, he laid the charge directly to her. "Why did you not answer my letters?"

Why? Because it would hurt too much if you never came back. Because dashed hopes are worse than no hope.

Or, at least, she had thought so. "I did write."

"Oh yes." He nodded sternly. "One letter, Lizzy. One letter."

She looked away, out into the trees.

He pulled a folded page of parchment from his pocket and set it on her lap. "One letter to warm a man's heart through all the trying nights of war. Here. Perhaps you would like to read your masterpiece."

She rubbed her thumb against the worn edges of the folded letter. She didn't have to read it. She knew the paltry sums included there. Just as Sir Godfrey had hidden his real purse, so Elizabeth had hidden her true thoughts, years ago, and handed Trace false words. Bland watery words, like weak unsalted soup. It pricked at her conscience, as sharply as if Trace held her at sword point. "I didn't think you would come back."

"What? And these were the sentiments you sent a dying man?"

"No. Not that!" She crumpled the letter. "I never thought you would be killed. I couldn't bear to think such things. No, I didn't believe you would ever come back *here*. To Claegburn." *Or to me. I thought you would break my heart. As if, when you left, the wretched thing didn't shatter anyway.*

"Uncle Adrian said you might aspire to great things. He explained that you had a brilliant future ahead of you." *A future that didn't include me.*

Trace held out his palm. "My letter."

She looked down at the wrinkled folds of paper in her lap, a humiliating testament to her stingy soul. "I would rather you didn't keep it."

He took it away from her and stuffed it back in his pocket.

They rode in silence to the Turners' hut and Elizabeth climbed down from the gig before he could help her. She carried the basket, making sure the small bag of coins stayed tucked securely under a loaf of bread.

Mary, the Turner's young daughter, ran out to greet them. The child was barefoot and clad only in a plain white shift in dire need of laundering. "Miss Whizzabess! What has you brung us?"

"Miss Elizabeth," Mary's mother corrected. Mrs. Turner straggled out of the house, her belly round as a melon, a lock of hair stringing down across her cheek, and a small boy clinging to one leg.

Elizabeth looped the basket through one arm and scooped up the eager little girl. "Good morning, Miss Mary." She smiled and tucked some of Mary's wild curls behind the child's tiny ears. "I've brought you fresh bread, and sausages, and lots of other delicious things from the ladies in the village. How is your mama today?"

Mrs. Turner chuckled from the doorway. "As well as can be expected, with one babe about to spring out and another one still wrapped around my leg. Tom is out in the fields, but he'll be back midday. Come in." She glanced quizzically at Trace.

Elizabeth performed the introductions.

The hut was small and dark. When Trace ducked under the lintel and entered, there seemed very little room left. Obviously, he would find no sign of the highwaymen here, only a cramped room, children in need of bathing, and a bench in the midst of repair.

"I'll finish this, shall I?" He took the rough-hewn leg and checked to see how snugly the new leg fit into the vacant hole on the bench. As she unpacked the sausages and chatted with Mrs. Turner, Elizabeth watched him covertly. He went out and dipped a cup into the rain barrel, and then returned to trickle water into the hole and around the edge of the joint.

When the water penetrated the wood of the leg, it would expand, causing it to stay firmly in place.

She and Trace stayed only a short while longer, time enough for Elizabeth to finish unloading the basket and discreetly hide the velvet bag behind the salt in Mrs. Turner's cupboard. She finished her work and handed little Mary a bright yellow lemon drop.

When they left, Trace turned north on the road through Claegburn Wood.

Elizabeth pointed the other way. "The Bernard farm is in that direction."

"A small detour."

"Through Claegburn Wood?"

He smiled. "So, you haven't entirely forgotten."

She said nothing, as the dogcart meandered deeper into the forest of beech trees with thickly twisted trunks and tall birches, creaking and bending in the slight breeze, leaves shivering and catching the sun like green-gold guineas.

"It hasn't changed much. Still beautiful." He glanced sidelong at her as if he included her in the compliment.

She took a deep breath. He didn't belong here. These were her woods now. He was a trespasser.

He spoke as casually as if they were sitting in the dower house parlor. "Sir Godfrey told my stepfather he heard music the night they were robbed. A flute, or so he thought."

Or was this simply casual conversation, or was he on the

hunt?

She glanced at him. "A flute? How very odd. It must have been his imagination. This is one of the old places. People are afraid druid spirits still roam these woods. It was dark. You know how the wind whistles through these trees."

Thou doth protest too much.

Elizabeth clamped her lips together and grimaced. She'd babbled worse than a guilty six year-old.

"Yes." He answered slowly, pensively, watching her carefully. "Those were my very thoughts, until I heard Blythe play that haunting melody yesterday, a tune very much like the one Godfrey described."

Elizabeth fought to moderate her breathing. "What can you mean? How can someone describe one tune enough to set it apart from another? It must be heard."

He shrugged, as if it were nothing. "I wondered if perhaps she plays the flute at night in the woods."

"Nana Rose would never allow such a thing."

He laughed to himself. "It wouldn't be the first time a young girl slipped out of the dower house to play in the woods at night."

She took in a quick breath. "I . . .you . . . that was different."

"Was it?" He turned the rig down a small path, overgrown from lack of traffic. "She might be meeting someone. A rendezvous."

"Blythe meeting with highwaymen? Bandits? I think not.

She's far too shy. The poor girl has scarcely ever spoken to a man aside from you and Lord Mulvern, and you've seen how reluctantly she speaks even then."

"Perhaps she only speaks to one particularly charming bandit. Someone who could ease her discomfort."

"No. Never. Blythe is not that sort of child. She would never—I know what you are thinking. But she is not like me, not nearly so reckless, or so foolish."

He stopped the dogcart by a tree. *Saints above. Their tree.*

She knew every tangled branch of that old beech by heart. Boughs had begun their life as separate fingers of the same root stretched upward seeking the light, twisting and coiling around one another until they all melded together to form one thick-knotted trunk.

Trace jumped down from the driver's bench and came for her, holding her too long as he lifted her down. "I promised I'd come back, Lizzy."

He didn't wait for an answer, but clasped her hand, pulling her beside him toward the thick old trunk, until they stood face to face, as they had so many years ago. He pressed her palm flat against the smooth white bark and covered it with his. "We promised. You should have believed me."

The ancient beech bark was the color of ashes burnt to whiteness, spent and dry, like her dreams. She slid her hand out from under his. "A child's promise. We were children."

"We were friends."

Yes. It was true. They'd been friends. Amidst all the turmoil, two lonely children clinging to their games and secret places, as if the ravages of death did not exist in these woods. "Companions in sorrow."

"More than that." His gaze pierced her through, sharp and knowing, spilling all her secrets into the air between them. "Much more than that."

She felt the need to run away and hide, as she had in the games they had played as children. "You left. You went away." Her accusing tone sounded harsher than she would have wished.

"To school. I had no choice. But at harvest-time, before my commission, do you not remember?"

Remember? Was he mad? How could she ever forget?

She might try. But Lucifer and all his demons would torment her eternally with the memory of that one luminous moment. One kiss that still scorched her soul. A kiss that meant everything, and then nothing, a kiss that smashed her heart to pieces when she heard the truth behind his urgency. He was leaving. Going off to war. Leaving her to serve king and country. She would only ever have that one kiss. "You left. Again."

"I told you I'd come back. And you promised—"

"That was four years ago, Trace." She turned away from him, leaning her forehead against the cool bark.

"You didn't believe me."

"Should I have? At one and twenty, I was already on the shelf. Most women of that age are married and have children. You left. You went away to build a life without me. Don't chide me for not waiting here under this wretched tree."

"I wrote to you. We were friends. I thought someday . . ."

"Someday?" She laughed softly. *"Someday* is a Banbury tale we tell children to lull them to sleep. You cast off Claegburn and all its grief. I couldn't fault you. If I'd been a man, I'd have done the same."

He toyed with the obstinate hairs at the base of her neck. "When you didn't write, I thought, perhaps, you'd met someone else."

She closed her eyes, pressing her head harder against the smooth bark, as if the old beech might hold the comfort of a mother's shoulder. "No. I've said my last prayers, Trace. I'm a spinster. I have my family to care for. The twins are the closest thing to children I will ever—"

"Lizzy, don't be foolish." He stroked the sides of her shoulders as if trying to warm her cold thoughts. "You're still vibrant and even lovelier than—"

"Don't." She spun, to face him. "I've heard all about the camp followers and the beautiful women in Spain."

He pressed his hands on the trunk on each side of her head, trapping her, bearing down on her. "I'm a man of my word, Lizzy. The intrigues of Napoleon's strategy occupied my nights, and the lives of my men consumed my days. I had no interest in camp followers. You should have written."

His mouth was a pawn's length from hers. She held her breath, unmoving. Afraid to hope. Afraid *not* to hope. Heaven above! Where was her sword when she needed it? If she had her sword, she might hold him hostage and extract everything she desired from him, all the lost words and missed touches. She would rob him of every kiss he owned, if only she had her sword. Instead, she was his hostage. Held captive by his nearness, his lips, his intoxicatingly masculine smell, and startlingly blue eyes that made long dead flames burn again.

His lips moved in a husky whisper. "I believe I will collect, now."

"Collect?" She gulped air, breaking the simple word into too many throaty syllables. Heat crawled up her neck and blazed onto her cheeks.

"Yes." His dimples deepened. "On your part of the bargain, of course."

He did not give her a chance to debate. He covered her mouth with his, softly stealing away four years of want. She opened to him, allowing him to fill her miserly heart with warmth. And now, she would have one more memory with which Lucifer would taunt her when she made her final journey to Hades.

Trace hugged her to his chest. "Lizzy, Lizzy, how I've missed you."

A tear escaped its mooring and glided down her cheek,

sliding, falling, like the last leaf of autumn. Glistening, it twirled down to crumble and rot beneath the tree, alongside the dreams that had fallen there four years ago. She'd made her choice, chosen a path that would divide them forever. Good from evil. He was an honest man. A gentleman of his word. She was a criminal. A thief. A liar. She had no future, save that which rightfully belonged to a hangman.

Sadly, gently, she pressed her hands against Trace's chest, separating them. "We have one last basket to deliver, and then I must return home. The twins ought to attend to their French lessons. Cook wants menus. The garden needs weeding."

Trace frowned, not an ordinary frown, but hard and intense, suddenly the soldier. She saw in his eyes questions roiling through his mind, questing for possible explanations.

If only he weren't such a strategist. Life is not a game. It does not come with a reliable set of rules. The knight doesn't always move two out and one over.

Trace hadn't.

And who in the blazes could ever predict what the queen would do? She climbed up into the rig and sat, hands folded primly in her lap.

Without further discussion, he maneuvered the dogcart back to the road. They delivered the basket to the Bernard family, and he helped her down at the dower house.

She was afraid to look him in the eye. "I'm sorry there

weren't any signs of the Frenchman."

"Far more than you might think, Lizzy." He tipped his hat and left her standing at the door.

Chapter 3

He Did Not Come In The Dawning
He Did Not Come At Noon

HE WAS NOT A FOOL. His conclusions were sound. It was the only explanation for her strange behavior. Trace stood at the corner of the bootmaker's, down the street from Mrs. Merton's boardinghouse, waiting.

He'd followed Elizabeth and Bertie as they'd made a furtive flight from the dower house the previous evening. He'd not expected the journey to end in London. He'd expected her to lead him to the highwayman's lair in a remote dell or thicket, hiding like a beast. Clever of the blighter to hide among the congested population of London. Even as Trace reluctantly admired the Frenchman's shrewdness, he hated him for it.

His jealousy constructed a dashing enigmatic rogue out of his adversary. *He must be deuced charming to lead Lizzy astray, to command her loyalty, and her secrecy. Robin Hood be damned. The Frenchman was simply a cunning thief! He charmed women while he robbed them. The scoundrel made a sport of frightening men. A thief! A reprobate bound for the gallows. Nothing more.*

Trace was certain Lizzy would come out. She would rendezvous with the black-hearted, highwayman. He was sure of it. Or, if she didn't, the unprincipled cur would come here to her. When he did, Trace would have him. After the highwayman danced his due on Tyburn's hanging tree, Lizzy would come to her senses.

To shield himself from the early morning drizzle, Trace pulled the collar of his greatcoat up. He would watch all day and all night if he had to. *Night.* Trace flexed his jaw muscles tight. *Just let the French devil show up at night. The hangman would not have to soil his rope.*

An hour passed. When the boardinghouse door opened, Trace prepared to dash around the corner, out of Lizzy's line of sight. Except it wasn't Lizzy. An elderly crippled woman emerged, assisted by a man, most likely her son.

ဆၣ

Lizzy hobbled toward Trace. She, an old crone, hunched, with a wadding hump fixed on her back, wearing miles of Nana Rose's black bombazine. From the dark depths of her poke bonnet, she watched, as the man she loved dismissed her and looked away. He didn't know her. She had half-hoped he would. Which was worse she wondered—that he would recognize her and expose her as a thief, or for her to be of so little consequence that she was invisible to him? The weight of the padding on her back felt heavier and she found it easy to drag her steps.

Lizzy sighed. *Old woman. That was all he saw.* As well he should, for she *was* old. Trace deserved a young, beautiful woman, one unfettered by the bondage of her crimes, one as true and decent as he was. A heroine. Not a villain.

Even so, he ought to have known her. Lizzy felt a compelling urge to rap him smartly with her cane as she shuffled past. In a low grumbling voice, Bertie, exercised her role as attentive son and urged Lizzy forward. "Come along now, mother."

Lizzy turned back for one last glimpse. He didn't even glance in their direction. Bertie tugged forcefully on her arm. They left him standing there in the mist, guarding the boardinghouse like a faithful sentry.

When they rounded the corner, Bertie hissed, "What are you playing at, my girl? He goes by the rules, that one. If he catches us, there's no saying he won't turn us in."

"Little doubt of it." Lizzy looked straight ahead. The poke bonnet acted as a blinder, shielding her from Bertie's inspection.

"Still in love with him, aren't you?"

Elizabeth was in no mood to pretend it wasn't so, or to ask foolish questions such as, *how did you know? She* shrugged. "What does it matter? It's impossible."

"Folderol."

"I'm too old."

"Balderdash."

"I'm a criminal," she whispered. "A robber. He's a war hero. He can't have a wife who deserves to go to the gallows."

Bertie shrugged. "He needn't know."

"He'd figure it out. One can't fool a man like Trace for long. He'd uncover the truth." Lizzy tugged at the black silk. "About this. About all of it. He'd know I deceived him."

"I daresay, he may find out anyway."

"Not if we're careful."

"Look here, Elizabeth." Bertie halted their progress and turned to face her. "I disagree. He's a first-rate fellow. If you want him, we'll all keep mum. No one ever need know about . . . the business."

"Lies? Between a husband and wife? It wouldn't be the honorable thing."

Honorable?

The irony choked her. She laughed, one dismal shudder. "Even if I could keep it from him, I'd live every day of my life wondering if, and when, the sword might fall."

Bertie blew out a ruff of air letting her lips ripple loudly.

"Then there's no way round it. It's a gamble, but you'll have to tell him the truth, straightway."

Elizabeth inhaled deeply. Hadn't she toyed with that very idea a thousand times? "No point. I know him. He wouldn't be able to stomach it. And I couldn't bear to see the look of disgust in his eyes. I'd rather hang."

Bertie didn't say anything more. It was one of the things Lizzy loved about Bertie. The woman knew when to be quiet. They walked the rest of the way to the jeweler's shop in silence.

The jeweler set his lens down on the black velvet cloth and shook his head. "A shame they aren't still in their original setting. Diamonds of this mediocre quality are worth far more mounted."

Bertie snarled low in her throat. "It was the only way my mother could get them out of France. In their settings, they're far too difficult to hide. Surely you must know this, yes?"

"Yes. Yes. Of course." The jeweler waved his hand dismissing the argument. "It is the same story with all the French émigrés. But what can I say?"

"How much?" Bertie demanded.

"One hundred pounds."

"Robbery, sir!"

"It is the going rate."

Lizzy spat out a string of vehement French oaths to Bertie, who nodded and turned back to the jeweler. "She says, she did not escape Madam Guillotine and her band of scurrilous swine to come here and have an Englishman cut her throat. Make a better offer, or we will go elsewhere."

"One hundred and thirty. That is my final bid." He folded his arms stubbornly.

Lizzy brusquely moved aside the jeweler's glass, gathered up the edges of the velvet, and tied a cord around the glittering pile of Sir Godfrey's wife's dismantled diamonds. She deposited the small bag into the recesses of her black bombazine and shuffled out of the store.

Their experience at the next jeweler's shop was only a moderate improvement. They trudged back to the boardinghouse, discouraged.

"Two hundred pounds." Lizzy lamented. "I had thought five hundred, at the very least."

"Skinflints. Miserly old gets. They'll sell those diamonds for three times that amount."

"Undoubtedly."

"What's the tally? Will we have enough to bring the twins out next season?"

"Not quite. It was going to be a scrape even if we'd gotten the five hundred."

"Could just bring out Bonnie."

"No! We agreed. Neither of them should have to molder away without a future. Blythe deserves a husband and children as much as Bonnie does. She may be quiet, but she still has the heart of a woman. She needs—"

"Very well." Bertie put up her hand to stem Lizzy's impassioned arguments. "You'll hear no complaint from me. One or two more midnight trysts should do it."

No complaint, indeed.

Lizzy frowned. Bertie's tone reflected altogether too much enthusiasm. "I don't like it. Not with Trace on the hunt." Lizzy inhaled deeply. "If only there was another way."

"Fiddle-faddle. More of a challenge. Half the fun is the game."

"Think of the risk. Not only for us, but the twins."

"Very well then. We'll leave them out of it. It'll just be the two of us. Better sport for us."

"Excessively difficult to deal with outriders with only two of us. Aside from that, if we're caught, the scandal alone would ruin Blythe and Bonnie's lives."

"We won't get caught."

"You underestimate Trace. He's tenacious. Thorough." Lizzy gestured toward the corner where he still stood guard on the boardinghouse. "Observe. He's still there."

Bertie chuckled. "I daresay he'll stand there all night."

"In this rain? What if he catches lung fever? I won't have that preying on my conscience as well. The sooner we leave, the sooner he'll go home, and get out of this merciless drizzle."

"Think, Lizzy. If we come to London and go nowhere, what

will he deduce?"

She sighed. "He might figure it out."

"Exactly right."

Elizabeth nodded. "We'd best do some shopping. Feathers for Nana Rose. Perhaps a fan for Lavinnia."

"I heard of a confectioner . . ." Bertie hesitated, a childlike expression lighting her aged features. "I would dearly love to try one of those new—"

"Ices from Gunter's." Lizzy beamed. "Precisely."

Trace rubbed at his neck, which was growing stiff from craning to watch the doorway down the road. He noted the elderly woman and her son returning to the boardinghouse. Still no sign of Lizzy. It wasn't like her to be a slug-a-bed. Where was she? Had the blasted *Frenchman* slipped past him somehow?

He was rewarded twenty minutes later. Elizabeth and Bertie walked out, opening a broad black umbrella, chatting like young girls, as carefree as pigeons in the king's park. He followed them to Piccadilly Street.

Admirable, Lizzy thought, how he followed at a distance, trying to blend in with the crowd, collar up, hat low. First, she and Bertie turned in to a shop and dickered with merchants over paste pearls for Blythe and Bonnie. Next, they went down the street to bargain for a silk fan for Lavinnia and a pair of ostrich feathers for Nana.

He was skilled at concealing himself, but it was impossible

for a man of Trace's stature and bearing to remain completely hidden. He may have dressed like every other man on the street, but his walk exuded authority and his posture clearly marked him as a peer of the realm. She knew where he was almost without looking. She could feel his presence and longed to draw near, but couldn't.

They strolled to Berkley Square for ices. Saddest of all was catching sight of him outside the window at Gunter's, his coat rain-soaked and his hat sodden. She hated that he should be out there in the murk, while they indulged in the delicious, sweet, lemony treat from inside the comfortable shop. "This is absurd. We should invite him in."

Bertie waved her spoon indecorously at Lizzy. "Can't do it, m'dear. Smash his male sensibilities to bits if he knew you'd spotted his game."

"He would adore this lemon ice. It's heavenly." Lizzy spooned up some of the delectable mixture.

"Let him see you enjoying it." Bertie laughed. "Serves him right for being so clever."

Chapter 4

Plaiting A Dark Red Love Knot Into Her Long Black Hair

The dower house overflowed with happy jabber and sighs of delight, as the women readied themselves for the false ball.

"You look magnificent, Nana." It was the first time in Lizzy's memory her grandmother had donned anything other than widow's garb.

Lord Mulvern hadn't sent a gown for Nana Rose, to which the grand dowager had snapped, "I don't need *his* charity. I have a perfectly good wardrobe of my own."

Indeed, her gown was a Georgian masterpiece, a full skirt with panniers of deep blue figured silk and a silver lace paneled front. With her white hair piled high, she looked like a queen from times past, albeit a queen without any jewelry.

Elizabeth was the last to ready herself. The candles on her

dressing table fluttered as she slid the gold sarcenet gown over her head. She watched in the mirror as the soft golden fabric shimmered gracefully, falling with feather light caresses over her breasts and hips, draping the curves of her body in spider web thin silk. The slippery fabric teased at her flesh, flaring the hunger that had been steadily mounting since the day Trace had taken her to Claegburn Wood.

He had kept his distance since then. Wise choice. Always so disciplined, Trace. She, on the other hand, had been left to the mercy of her lurid imagination, an impish portion of her vile brain, relentless in its wicked desire to drive her mad with unattainable cravings.

For this one night, she would pretend she was an alluring princess, a woman free to follow her heart. A seductress. He would pay for making her want him again.

"Helen of Troy." Blythe stood in the doorway. "You look like her."

"That's very kind of you to say." Elizabeth smiled. "Would you help me with these ties, dearest?"

Thin ropes of gold crisscrossed Grecian-style over Lizzy's breasts. Blythe deftly wound the cords over the fabric and tied them in back, murmuring as she worked. "Troy fell. Greeks plundered the city. Paris was slain and Hecabe howled in grief. All because of Helen of Troy."

Perhaps it had not been a compliment, after all. "Are you worried about this evening, Blythe?"

"Grandmother has made pockets. Bertie's reticule is too big. It's a Trojan horse."

What in heaven's name did Blythe mean? Were these unfounded fears? Anxiety? *Or could it be that Blythe was the only one in the house with any sense?* Trace's parting words echoed in Lizzy's ears. He had guessed something, but what? He'd followed them to London, but why? Were they in danger of discovery? Perhaps, but not tonight.

"Blythe, darling, you're right. There is a Trojan horse tonight. That's what you must be sensing. My darling girl, you needn't worry. The Trojan Horse will be outside. A coach, full of armed men, sent to flush out the highwaymen. They will be out on the roads, riding up and down, hoping to snare us. But we will be safe, seated at Lord Mulvern's table having a lovely dinner and listening to music. Do you see?"

Blythe lowered her eyes. She didn't look comforted.

Lizzy hugged her. "It will be as sweet and uneventful as a Sunday pudding. I promise."

Twenty minutes later, Lord Mulvern's coach arrived to collect the ladies of the dower house. It was impossible to squeeze all six of them into the carriage.

"Do try to scoot over a little farther, Rose." Lavinnia wriggled herself onto the seat next to her mother-in-law. Nana Rose's hoops bulged so high that Lavinnia was almost hidden behind them. "If you will, kindly pull the cord and bunch up your panniers."

Their grandmother remained primly posed on the seat, her white pompadour wedged against the ceiling, bending her new ostrich feathers so far forward they almost tickled her nose. And yet she did not budge an inch. "The hinge is broken."

"It won't do." Bertie stood outside the coach, her arms folded stubbornly. "Too cramped. Not to mention—I can't breathe in there. There's enough flower petal perfume to suffocate a beehive."

Nana Rose scowled at her daughter. "Don't be ridiculous. You can't ride on the roof like a man."

"Can and will." Bertie pulled up the hood of her cape and turned to the footman. "Don't stand there like a jackass. Help me up onto the box."

Without displaying even the slightest inkling of astonishment, the very proper footman aided and abetted the recalcitrant Bertie, who was bound to be a great deal more comfortable on the driver's seat beside a scandalized coachman than crammed into the coach with the rest of them. Fortunately, it was a short journey to Lord Mulvern's home.

Elizabeth hadn't been back to Claegburn Manor in many months. The house always brought back a flood of memories from when she and her parents had lived there, the days when her father had been Lord of Mulvern.

Each of the women, except the twins, remembered their sojourn in the house. Although it was better not to think of those days, how could they not? The very sound of their feet on the marble, the curve of the staircase, the quality of light glittering from the chandelier—every small detail evoked images from days long lost. Departed fathers, brothers, sons . . . these women also keenly recalled the Claegburn men, who had sojourned there with them.

Elizabeth could still see her mother smiling at her from the drawing room, her father standing by his study door at the end of the hallway. Trace running down the stairs, his mother reprimanding him for his haste. Ghosts, all. Save one.

Would he be here tonight? Or, was Trace out riding with the ruse coach, waiting to ambush and capture the Frenchman and his band of rogues? She hoped not. She had an ambush of her own planned, schemes and traps, a dozen little torments she intended to practice on him. Let him discover the anguish of wanting something, someone, beyond his reach.

Bonnie, who had no weighty memories dragging at her feet, pattered gaily up the stairs, close behind the butler, leading the way up to the dining room. Elizabeth quietly reminded her cousin that Nana Rose must enter first.

"The Dowager Lady Mulvern," the butler announced with a flourish.

Nana Rose paraded into the ballroom with her head erect. A bittersweet mask hid the turmoil Lizzy knew her grandmother felt at being announced as a guest in what had been her own home.

Bonnie leaned forward and peeked around the doorjamb, giggling at her grandmother's stately entrance. Lizzy pulled the pink minx back where she belonged and sent her a silent scold. The girl must learn to watch her manners before they took her to London for a season.

The butler announced Lavinnia, who strode amiably into the room. Shorter than Trace's mother had been, Lavinnia had cleverly altered the green silk gown, giving it an elegant train.

Lizzy would like to have seen Lord Mulvern's face when he saw Lavinnia. From the hallway, they heard his gruff voice ring out satisfyingly. "Lavinnia! 'Pon my word, you look quite handsome."

Bonnie hid her mirth behind her hand, her golden curls jounced in adorable perfection. She would do well in London, even without much of a dowry. Bonnie, at least, would not spend her life a spinster, as Elizabeth and Bertie must do. Neither would Blythe, if Lizzy had anything to do with it.

Blythe looked like a fairy princess captured from Claegburn Wood and dragged into the light against her will. Beautiful, but desirous of escape.

"You needn't worry," Lizzy whispered, trying to reassure her.

"Lady Bertilde Claegburn," the butler called. Bertie squared her shoulders and marched into the room like a general come to inspect the troops.

Lizzy's turn next.

She floated into the ballroom, ready to snare her conquest. Candles blazed along the walls. Musicians played sedately at the far end of the room. Lord Mulvern waited, Aunt Lavinnia at his side, and another gentleman, but not Trace.

Lizzy couldn't help it. She looked desperately around the room. Empty chairs. Familiar faces in paintings on the wall. The one face she wanted to see was missing. No Trace. Of course not, and why would he be here? To see her? Ha! The wretch. He was out in the woods, hunting his beloved Frenchman. She was a silly mooncalf for thinking it would have been otherwise. She struggled to school her features.

Elizabeth curtsied. "Thank you for inviting us, Uncle Adrian."

"Pleasure, Lizzy." Lord Mulvern took her hand and bowed over it graciously. "I've a surprise for you, young ladies. A dancing master." He pointed to the gentleman at his left elbow. "From London. After I hired the musicians, I thought to myself—waste of money if the gels don't know how to dance. Mr. Bledsoe, here, will show us all the latest dances, eh?"

The dancing master bowed with a flourish.

She knew how to dance. Although, it was probably not the ideal time to tell Lord Mulvern that she and his stepson had practiced dancing under a midnight moon in Claegburn

Wood. No, decidedly not. "That will be lovely. Most thoughtful. Thank you."

"Yes, indeed. Most generous." Lavinnia smiled. "Just as I've always said."

"Tut tut, nothing to it. Shall we dine now and enjoy dancing after?"

Bonnie smiled eagerly. "By all means."

The footman threw open the doors. The magnificent dining room sparkled with silver and glass. Lord Mulvern's servants brought forth a sumptuous feast, surpassing even Bonnie's expectations. Or so the young lady declared with unbridled enthusiasm. "Beef! Oh, Uncle Adrian. It is even more delicious than I remembered."

Elizabeth toyed with the coveted roast beef, rearranging it on her plate. Disappointment filled her stomach, leaving little room for this evening's delicacies, no matter how long awaited. She glanced across the table and caught Bertie in the act of secreting a large slice of beef into her lap. No doubt the beef was destined for deposit in the 'too big' reticule Blythe had mentioned. Egad! Judging by the satisfied gleam on Bertie's countenance, the beef was not the first item to make a furtive passage into the depths of her bag.

Lizzy grimaced as more meat continued to disappear. She fervently hoped the servants were too busy to notice. During dinner, several slices of ham, a loaf of cheese, three apples, four dried spiced pears, and a half-dozen sculptured sugar confections found their way to Bertie's portable pantry under the table.

When, at last, dinner ended and they filed out of the dining room, Elizabeth fell in step beside Bertie. "I'm surprised you can carry your bag without assistance."

Bertie grinned, unashamed.

Lizzy inhaled her chagrin and whispered. "Good gracious. Are you not afraid it will drip?"

Bertie hefted the enormous purse. "I lined it with oil cloth. She's as watertight as a ship's hull."

Another odd-shaped ship, Nana Rose, sailed ahead of them, floating across the ballroom floor like a petite blue galleon. Nana glided directly out of the gaily-lit room to ports unknown. *She's up to something.* Lizzy started to follow her mischievous grandmother, but Bonnie waylaid her. "Lizzy, you must come and make up our set. You and Bertie will make six. Blythe won't dance. She insists on watching the musicians."

At the far end of the room, Blythe had positioned a chair beside the trio of musicians, where she would, undoubtedly, sit and study every movement. Elizabeth dearly wished she might sit beside her young cousin and do nothing, think nothing, and feel nothing. If she had her way, she would sit and simply allow the music to transport her to a soothing place filled with carefree fantasies.

Bonnie tugged her hand, pulling her into the middle of the

room, where the dancing instructor led them in the steps of a *Danse Ecossoise*. It was so remarkably similar to a country-dance, Lizzy would have sworn he was making up the steps as they went along. After the vigorous romp, their instructor suggested they learn the more sedate, if rather more scandalous, steps of the waltz.

Lord Mulvern cleared his throat. "Now see here, young man, that's not quite the thing for genteel young ladies."

The very elegant instructor took no affront. His hand revolved gracefully as he made each of his points, and explained that even the esteemed patronesses of Almack's had sanctioned the waltz. "All the most elegant and fashionable balls in London boast of a waltz or even two. It is essential for the young ladies to know the steps, lest they appear provincial."

Lord Mulvern sputtered. "Very well. Mustn't be backward." He tried to disguise his bruised dignity and lined up beside Lavinnia. "Show us this infamous waltz."

The dancing master took a position next to Elizabeth and lifted her hand in his. At his nod, the musicians began to play in three-four time. "It is a simple square pattern, like so."

It took Elizabeth a few minutes to adapt to the correct steps. Once she did, it was a comfortable easy rhythm.

Blythe rose from her chair and stood in front of the musicians shaking her head, her hands to her ears. There was a disturbance as the fellow with the violin lost his place and stopped playing, obviously exasperated with his critic. After a whispered argument, Blythe took the instrument he thrust at her and fell in beside the other musicians.

Lizzy almost stumbled as her cousin put bow to the strings. The first strains were awkward and squawky, but in a trifling, the most beautiful sounds she had ever heard flowed from the violin. Long, deep, reverberating arpeggios arced up like a rainbow to meet quick high staccato chords. The waltz took on a new character, full of passion, almost mystical in its power to control Lizzy's own heartstrings. "Remarkable," she murmured.

As the dancing master led Elizabeth in a turn, completing the square pattern, she nearly lost her breath. A gentleman stood in the doorway. His gaze fixed on her. Trace!

He strode into the room, halted Lord Mulvern's waltz with Lavinnia, and whispered in his stepfather's ear. Lord Mulvern nodded gravely and turned back to find his step with Lavinnia.

Music echoed around the nearly empty ballroom. Yet, she heard each of Trace's footfalls report on the wood floor, marked each footstep coming closer, growing louder, until at last, he stopped at her side. He tapped the dancing master's shoulder. "If I may?"

The dancing master bowed without a word and handed Lizzy into Trace's arms.

She smiled, pleased beyond her ability to hide it. "I'm

afraid you will have to be patient with me. I'm not very adept at the waltz yet."

His face remained grave. Implacable. "I'm sure you will catch on quickly enough."

She felt self-conscious under his stern scrutiny. Where was the flattery she had expected? The yearning in his eyes? He spun her deftly around the room.

She tried to draw him out. "I see you've waltzed before."

"Visiting dignitaries. Military balls. Would you have expected anything less?"

Lizzy's ancestors' faces were a blur as she whirled dizzily past the paintings on the wall. Trace took long confident steps, waltzing her at far too vigorous a pace around the room. His chest expanded and contracted heavily, although, she guessed, it had little to do with the exertion of the dance.

As they approached the open doors to the balcony, without missing a step, he whisked her out into the darkness.

Chapter 5

One Kiss, My Bonnie Sweetheart, I'm After a Prize Tonight

The air was cool and sweet. Lord Mulvern's untended gardens bloomed profusely with wildflowers and gangly remnants of the garden's former glory.

Trace suited the width of his steps to the narrow balcony. The hand, which he had held with rigid correctness on her shoulder, slid lower, into the small of her back. He pulled her closer. "You didn't ask me if I caught the highwayman."

Fool! She was a fool. She'd forgotten. She'd only thought of claiming his attention. Of luring him. Of tantalizing him into one more kiss. She regulated her breathing and tried her best to appear calm. "If you had, you would be jubilant, wouldn't you? I can tell by your demeanor, he escaped."

"Escaped?" Trace laughed derisively. There was no humor

in his eyes. "The coach went up the road. Circled round on side roads. Then came up the main road again. And again. Five men hired, three waiting with guns in the coach, and it goes round and round like a child's top."

He clutched her closer. The music took on a subtle quality as they moved farther away from the doors. They were almost to the edge of the balcony, where roses meandered haphazardly up the stone walls. "Tell me the truth, Lizzy."

Her feet faltered. "What do you mean?"

He caught her, supporting her in his arms, his face dangerously close. "The Frenchman. You warned him away, didn't you?"

"No." She shook her head. "I didn't. Why would you think that?"

"But, you *do* know him."

"No."

"You're lying. I see it in your eyes. I know you too well." He brushed a strand of hair out of her face, smoothing his fingers across her cheek. "You're lying. Not only that, I can tell you're afraid. But of what? Is he your lover?"

"*Are you mad?*" She tried to pull out of his arms, but he held her in place.

"You may as well confess, Lizzy. That day in the woods, I figured it out."

"What are you saying?"

"The kiss. I knew you still loved me. I could feel it. Still feel it. The way you look at me. When I touch you . . . I can tell. Except you keep pushing me away. There can be only one explanation. The despicable cur has some hold over you."

"No."

"Someone warned him away. I followed you to London. Did you meet him there? A rendezvous? Did a note pass between you? Tell me!"

"No. You don't understand." She backed up, groping for the wall, grasping for something solid to hold onto.

"Then make me understand." He grabbed her shoulders, forcing her to look him in the eyes. "I'll believe you if you'll just tell me the truth."

If only she could tell him. Her anguish must have spoken too fluently. He tried to answer for her.

"Give me another explanation. Is it that you depend upon the money he leaves you? Has Bonnie or Blythe succumbed to his charm? A man like that would be a grave temptation for a young naive girl. Or did he charm you?" He stopped scrambling for an answer and searched her face.

She felt herself shaking. Desperate not to lie. Equally desperate not to be found out.

"You're shaking. I've frightened you." He searched her face and remorse twisted his features. "Forgive me, my dearest." He loosened his grip. "I'm a fool. Jealousy muddled my thinking. You're right—I've gone mad wondering what you're hiding." He raked a hand over his forehead, scraping back his hair as if it might rub away his misgivings. "What was I thinking? You would never consort with a thief. I should've known better. Not you."

If only it were consorting.

His words landed on her chest like heavy stones, crushing her. She feared to breathe. It took every ounce of her strength to force herself to speak, a feather light petition that meant life or death. "What then, could you never love a thief?"

"A thief? Of course not." He smirked, as if she jested with him.

So certain of his answer.

She wanted to weep. He would never love a thief. Of course not. It was Trace, loyal and true, above reproach. She'd known the answer before she'd dared to ask. Fortunately, he still held her, because her legs had no more will to perform their task. She found it difficult to call the blood up from her heart, or force air into her lungs. It no longer mattered.

"Lizzy, what's wrong?" He held her chin in his fingers. "Tell me the truth?"

The truth? I am the despicable cur. I am the unlovable thief. There is your truth.

She struggled to be free of those eyes that peered so easily into her soul. What a fool she'd been to think she could come here and pretend, *even for one night*, that she was worthy of his affection. "I can't."

"If he ruined you, I'll . . ."

What would you do? Kill the Frenchman? She had a mad urge to laugh. Scream. Run. Instead, all emotion drained from her, like blood from a mortal wound.

"Is that it? Hear me, Lizzy. I won't let you throw your life away for a man with no scruples. A scoundrel. A . . ." He damned her with every harsh word he spoke against his enemy. His eyes, those wretchedly earnest eyes, implored her to answer. "Give him up, my darling. Tell me the truth."

She tried to look away, but he held her tight and chased her soul. Harried, she spat what little truth she could at him, "I don't know a French man. None! Not a single one."

"Lizzy, please. I don't care what he's done to you. It doesn't matter. Do you hear? You belong to me. With me. You always have."

When she didn't respond, he let go and waited. A thousand miles away, inside Lord Mulvern's ballroom, the waltz played on. In the garden, crickets rasped a dull accompaniment. High above a beech tree in the woods, an owl screeched his shrill hunting cry and silent rabbits shivered in fear.

Trace lifted a coil of her dark hair that had fallen across her breast, and held it loosely in his fingers. "Come back to me, Elizabeth." He kissed her then, with the soft sweet sadness of one saying farewell to a dying friend.

If this was to be her last touch from him, she would have more.

Lizzy circled her arms around his neck, drawing him in,

kissing him not as a corpse, but as the wicked wanton thief she was, stealing as much of his heart as he would allow.

A low rumble in his throat warned her that she'd dared too much. He pulled her against his chest, plundering her mouth, even as she ravaged his. No tender kisses. He made penetrating demands on her mouth, which meant, *these lips belong to me.* He kissed her with so feverish an intensity he may as well have declared aloud, *Elizabeth, you belong to me—body and soul.*

Trace stopped abruptly and stepped away from her, his breath ragged. "How can you give yourself to me so freely, and yet withhold from me the truth?"

She lowered her eyes. Moonlight glinted off the gold strands in her gown. "Because, the truth is far worse than you imagine."

She would never forget his face, how it looked in that moment. How the color drained, and even in the darkness he looked pale. His pain turned to outrage, and finally vengeance. She knew then, he was lost to her forever.

He backed away, pointing at her, as if he had finally identified his enemy. "Then, I *will* kill him. I swear it!"

He left her standing there, bracing herself against the wall. The perfume of roses and wild honeysuckle floated on the black breeze, like a curse. Sweetness, where there should only be bitterness. "You are too late," she whispered to the wind. "I am already dead."

Slowly, Lizzy walked back to the ballroom. As she came through the door, Nana Rose bumped into her, clinking like teacups tossed in a flour sack.

"What happened?" her grandmother demanded in a hushed voice. "I was coming to find you. Something's amiss. Trace stormed into the ballroom just now looking as if he meant to chew a lion in half."

"Nothing. Leastwise, it's nothing that can be helped." Lizzy took Nana Rose by the elbow and guided her toward the hallway. "Come with me to the retiring room. Surely you realize you're rattling?"

"It's these hinges."

"I sincerely doubt it."

She maneuvered Nana into the sitting room across the hall and shut the door behind them. "Show me."

"Show you what? Are you foxed? Must have been that strong wine at dinner. You're talking nonsense."

Lizzy lifted aside one of the overskirts draping Nana's pannier. "Pockets. Very clever."

Nana Rose sniffed defensively.

Lizzy sighed. "What did you take?"

"You, of all people, ought not scold me."

"I'm not scolding."

Reluctantly, Nana Rose pulled wide the pouch hanging inside the hooped framework of her skirt.

Lizzy peeked inside and looked up, open-mouthed, at her

prim and proper grandmother. "Candlesticks?"

Nana shrugged. "Silver. And I'll have you know, that snuffbox belonged to my Royce. So don't say another word about it."

"And in the other side?"

Nana grumbled but opened the other pannier for inspection.

Lizzy's shoulders sagged. "A vase? Aren't you afraid it will be in pieces by the time we get home?"

"Don't be silly. That's why I wrapped the table runner around it. Embroidered that runner myself. Only proper I should have it back."

Nana Rose picked up a tortoiseshell hairbrush.

"Do you remember this brush? I used it a hundred times during those years." She tucked the brush inside the vase.

Lizzy shook her head. "With that in there, you're bound to rattle even louder."

"Wretched entailment." Nana Rose yanked a fringed damask cover from off a small side table and packed it around the brush and vase. *"The house and all its accoutrements. . .* Men write those idiotic things. It's enough to rip a woman's heart out."

"I believe it is time we took our leave for the evening."

Grandmother looked longingly around the room. "Yes. Take me away, Lizzy, before I cannot walk for carrying things."

Lavinnia burst into the room, fanning herself with the new silk fan. "Waltzing. It's wonderful. Lovely. I daresay, I'm completely winded."

Nana Rose hurriedly adjusted her overskirt to hide the pockets.

Bertie strolled in behind Lavinnia, lugging her reticule. "I've had my fill of dancing." She glanced warily from Rose to Lizzy. "Ho now, what's to do in here?"

"I'll tell you what's to do. I've exciting news." Lavinnia fanned herself, grinning like a delighted child. "Lord Mulvern is convinced the Frenchman and his band of thieves are routed. After tonight, they know they're being hunted. They won't dare risk another robbery. He's going to invite Lord Loughton and several of his old friends and their wives for a weekend of hunting and cards. And the best part is—he invited *me* to act as his hostess. Oh, we'll have music and feasting. Isn't it wonderful?"

"Perfect." Bertie's face fairly danced with predatory eagerness.

One last time and then they were done. Judging by the excitement on Bertie's face, it might prove harder to give up their midnight trysts than Lizzy had expected.

"Wonderful. If you like that sort of thing." Nana Rose headed for the door, sagging like a weather-beaten ship. "Time we took our leave."

Late that night, after they'd gone back to the dower house

and all the Claegburn women had settled in their beds, Lizzy blew out her candle and sat beside her window. She knew Trace was out there. Felt it. She strained to see into the darkness, trying to discern shadowy shapes in the woods above the house. He would keep watch for *The Frenchman*, laboring under the misbegotten notion that the illusive highwayman would ride up to her window for a moonlit assignation.

Go to him. Her feckless heart throbbed commands. *Run to the woods. Find him. Tell him the truth.*

If he led her to the gallows, so be it. What good was her life without him?

Except she didn't have the right to bring consequences down upon Bertie's head. Nor could she ruin Blythe and Bonnie's future. Or shame her grandmother any further. She stood facing the window with her head bowed.

ഇരു

The moon waltzed with the dark swirling clouds. Trace leaned against a creaking birch on the rise above the dower house. From here, no one could reach the house without his knowing. She stood in her window, taunting him, white angelic night rail, her black hair tumbling over her shoulders. He ached for her.

Come to me, Lizzy,

She must know he was here. She looked out into the forest as if she could see him. *Come out We will waltz under the old beech. I'll hold you forever, if only you will come to me.*

Or, was she waiting for the Frenchman?

Devil take the bastard. Let him show his swarthy face anywhere near Lizzy and blood would flow.

Chapter 6

When the Road Is a Ribbon of Moonlight,
The Highwayman Comes Riding

Two weeks later

The midnight moon galloped high above the trees. From the rise, Trace followed the progress of Lord Loughton's borrowed coach as it turned down the secluded road into Claegburn Wood. His edgy outrider hung back, warily watching his flanks. Deeper into the thick forest the coach went, making it difficult for Trace to follow its movements.

They would strike soon, The Frenchman and his band of thugs. Trace nudged his horse down into the dense woods, hoping his mount's cautious steps would not alert the highwaymen. Through the trees, he caught glimpses of the amber coach lamps bobbing and flickering as the coach moved forward, a flash of reflected light from the harness metal, a glimmer of brass on the top rail.

A muffled cry. *The game had begun.*

Trace urged his horse to a quicker pace and approached the road. A furlong behind the coach, Trace found his fallen outrider lying in the road, thrashing about like an overgrown carp, cinched securely in a fishing net, with a rag jammed in his mouth.

Trace couldn't take the time to free his incompetent sentry. He distinguished the outline of the coach, standing still. Dismounting, Trace crept nearer, closing in on the bandits.

Only two? Where was the band of cutthroats?

He'd heard tales of black-clad thieves dropping from the sky, as numerous as gutter rats, swarming over hapless coaches. Only two. He could take two by himself. One rogue in particular held his interest. The Frenchman.

Elizabeth, having dispatched the outrider, approached the coach, ready to throw open the door. Before she could reach it, the latch handle clicked and turned. The door creaked slowly open, the nostrils of a twin-barreled flintlock leading the way. Through the glass, she recognized the nervous face of one of Lord Mulvern's stablemen.

She saw it all then. Trace had beaten her at her own game. Checkmate. She slammed the carriage door against the stable lad's hand. He yipped. The pistol fell to the ground and discharged.

"Trap!" She yelled. "Run!" She scooped up the weapon and threw it into the bushes.

Footsteps thudded behind her. She turned. Black, his silhouette in the moonlight, yet she knew him. Knew he would follow her. He wanted The Frenchman. Bertie, securing the coachman, leapt down from the box and headed north, into the deep woods. Lizzy would go south, giving her aunt a chance to escape.

Like a frightened doe, she charged uphill, crashing through underbrush, dashing between trees. A thicket—she needed a thicket in which to hide. Birches sparkled white in the moonlight. The ground, a dull gray carpet of leaves. Too bright— she needed the dark of a moonless night Treacherous silver beams slashed through the canopy of branches, illuminating the hunted.

The sound of snapping branches, whipping saplings warned her of his closeness. Night creatures scattered, pattering up trees and rustling out of their path. Her heart flapped and fluttered like a wild imprisoned bird.

The clap of gunshot alarmed her, but she was certain he had missed. A bullet would have dropped her. *Surely*. The fire scorching through her shoulder must have been a stab from a sharp branch. She stumbled but regained her balance and kept plowing forward. A cave. A ravine. A cleft in which to hide. But there was none.

Pain spread to her lungs, making breathing an agony. She

clutched her shoulder, but, through her glove, felt only the vague sensation of heat. She leaned against a sturdy beech. A copse, too dense for passage, lay ahead. Her vision blurred. *Which way? Which way?* Left, too open. Right, too steep.

She needed air. *Breathe.*

The world wobbled crazily.

His boots behind her—crushing leaves, breaking sticks. He was upon her. She wheeled around in time to meet his second shot. See a tiny red spark. Hear the echoing blast.

ഇൻ‌ൽ

The rogue's impertinent tricorn lay in the leaves, the feather fluttering frivolously in the wind. Let it lie there and rot. Debris. Rubbish.

Trace nudged the fallen highwayman with the toe of his boot. *It moaned.*

Intending to put the cur out of his misery, Trace aimed his pistol at the rascal's forehead. A forehead that began to look oddly familiar.

No!

Sudden fear rushed through him, colder than ice, burning and scorching its way into his gut.

No! It couldn't be.

He shook his head, dropped to his knees and ripped away the black eye mask. "God in heaven. No!" He yanked at the scraggy beard and discovered strings held it in place. "Lizzy! No. No. No!" Untying it, he cast the ruddy thing in the leaves.

He grabbed her shoulders and lifted her into his lap. It felt like warm clotted cream oozing over his fingers. Blood.

Trace ripped open her blouse to find the flow and stop it. A breastplate of wood, overlaid with thick tin, covered her chest. He saw then the remains of his ball lodged in the protector directly over her heart. Compulsively, he touched the indentation. At least that shot had not found its mark completely. Gray moonlight illuminated his bloody fingers. They looked black in the dim light, blood, black as sin, black as death.

He pulled her shirt off farther and found the source of the bleeding. His first shot had not missed. He snatched out his handkerchief and pressed it over the wound in her shoulder.

What had he done?

God, help her. God, help him. He couldn't live with himself if he'd killed her.

She moaned, her face as pale and ashen in the moonlight. Gray as the beech under which she lay. "Lizzy."

Her eyelids fluttered. Recognition flitted briefly in her eyes. "Take me home." She looked away. "To Nana."

He pulled off his neckcloth and wrapped it tightly around her chest and shoulder. She cried out when he lifted her up to his horse, but then lay silent in his arms as he rode to the dower house.

Lizzy, the highwayman? A criminal? A thief?

He couldn't comprehend it. Yet, he should have guessed. All the clues were there. He should have known.

London. The old woman and her son. She'd tricked him. Walked brazenly past him. Deceived him, but not in the way he'd expected. All the pieces spun into place. He wanted to roar like an injured lion, howl his pain at the moon. What a fool she must think him.

Deceit. He hated it.

Even so, he couldn't bring himself to hate her. He looked at the stranger collapsed in his arms, the woman he thought he knew so well, but didn't know at all. She, nearly dead from his bullet. It would be so much easier if he *could* hate her. Her treachery pierced him through, as lethal as a gunshot.

Middle of the night, the dower house should be quiet and dark. Instead, the windows flickered with candlelight. Old ladies and young women were running about as if it was midday. He supposed they were all in a panic. The door flew open as he rode up.

Nana Rose ran out in her night rail. "What have you done? Is she dead? You fiend! Murderer! How could you do this? How could you kill my dear sweet girl?"

Bertie, still dressed in highwayman-black, ran out beside the old woman. "Hush, Mother. He didn't know."

The twins rushed out and stopped short at the sight of Lizzy collapsed in his arms. Nana Rose turned and clung to

Bonnie, weeping.

Bertie hurried to his horse and reached for Lizzy's lifeless body, helping Trace hold her steady as he climbed down. Bertie whispered. "Is she . . .?"

Trace shook his head. "Still breathing, but unconscious."

Females flocked around as he carried Lizzy into the house. He followed Bertie up the stairs to Elizabeth's bedroom. The women traipsed behind him like a parade of grim mourners until Nana Rose came to her senses and started shouting orders to the entire household.

"Heat some water. Bonnie, bring me a thin sharp knife. Maggie, build a fire in her room. Rags! We'll want plenty of rags. Needles. Catgut. Find some brandy or port. There must be some alcohol around here somewhere. And salve. Lavinnia, get the laudanum. Blythe, I'll need your steady hands."

Trace laid Lizzy on clean white sheets. A dark red stain fanned out under her shoulder. "I'll go for a physician."

"Can't!" Bertie ordered as she hurriedly built a fire. "The sawbones won't keep mum."

"Shooting our Lizzy wasn't enough?" Nana Rose nudged Trace out of the way. "You wish to see her hanged as well?" The old woman carefully untied the makeshift breastplate and removed it.

Bertie stared at Trace, troubled. "Best to come straight out and tell us what's in the cards. Not much sense patching her up for the gallows. Too much grief, that way."

He turned away from Bertie's question, back to the woman he had loved. Lizzy lay dying, a thin chemise barely concealing her breasts.

Pale enticing flesh. Red alarming blood. Sweet sinful black tresses. Pure white linen. His jaw tightened so fiercely his head hurt. *Black or white?*

If he didn't awaken from this nightmare, madness would take him. He raked a hand into his hair, trying to hold onto his reeling mind. Suddenly, the air seemed to grow thin in the room. He forced himself to breathe, to cling to the things that kept his world tilted upright.

The fire began to crackle. Nana Rose put the knife into the flame. Bertie awaited his answer.

He took one last look at Elizabeth Claegburn before he spoke. "For all your sakes, I will not report any of this. But neither can I traffic in lies. Lord Mulvern is a good man. The only father I've ever known. I cannot stay in the vicinity and fail to tell him the truth. I'll take my leave on the morrow. Your secret will be safe."

Bertie nodded.

Nana Rose's shoulders sagged with relief.

"Now, we must get on with this." His voice sounded hollow, like someone giving orders from far away. "I'll hold her down while you clean and cauterize the wound."

"Won't do." Rose shook her head, and spoke with more compassion in her voice than Trace had ever heard in it before. "We have to remove her clothes. You'd best be on your way. We know what to do."

"For pity's sake, you can't stand on decorum. I'm not leaving until I know she's in the clear. You'll need help holding her. Believe me, I've seen this procedure often enough on the battlefield."

Bertie moved protectively in front of the bed. "Not done to a woman, you haven't."

Nana thrust her fists on her hips. "Not to my grand-daughter."

Blythe floated into the room like a benign ghost, carrying salve and needle and thread. "No point arguing with Nana. She's a mind like granite. Jagged and unyielding."

"Exactly." The old woman came at Trace like a cantankerous goat, head down, ready to butt or shove him out of the room. "And the sooner you leave, the sooner we can tend her wound." She grabbed hold of his arm and pushed him toward the door.

He stood firm. "This is nonsense. I've known her since we were in leading strings."

"A shame you didn't know her well enough not to shoot her." Nana glared at him. "And unless you want her to bleed to death, I suggest you find your way out the door." She pointed emphatically.

He shook his head. *Stubborn old woman.* "Who here has the strength to hold her down? Neither of you. She will fight, believe me. Which of you has the nerve to dig in her flesh and find the ball?"

Blythe, unblinking, completely calm, looked up at him. "I will remove the bullet."

Bertie clapped him on the shoulder. "Bonnie and I can hold her down. Tie her, if we have to. Don't worry, lad. We'll manage."

Bertie maneuvered him to the doorway, shoving him out of the way. Bonnie rushed into the room holding a bottle aloft. "Found some brandy! Mother's coming with the laudanum."

He hesitated in the doorway beside Bertie. "You're certain you can manage? I don't like it."

"Quite certain," Bertie assured him.

"One request. If she should . . ." He couldn't bring himself to say it.

"Die?" Nana Rose frowned impatiently at him, "Hurry up— leave and she won't."

"If you would send word to me through my father. I—"

"Of course." Bertie nodded gravely.

He left the room so the women could get on with their task. From the bottom of the stairs, he heard Lizzy moaning. As he reached the front door, she cried out in such anguish he had to clutch the doorframe, gripping it so tight his knuckles turned white. It was all he could do not to turn around and run back up those stairs. Naked or not, she needed him.

Oh, yes. She needed the man who shot her.

Trace had not cried since his mother died. The turmoil in his heart threatened to undo him. Lavinnia walked up behind him and quietly rested her hand on his bowed shoulder. Ever the optimist, she made a feeble attempt to placate him. "All will be well. You'll see."

Except it would *not* be well. *Nothing would ever be right again.*

Lizzy screamed. Her agony ripped him wide open. Trace stumbled out into the darkness to find his horse, tears washing down his cheeks.

Chapter 7
Shot Down Like a Dog in the Highway

AT MIDDAY, Trace set out in his stepfather's coach, heading to his mother's family estate in Northampton. He had intended to sleep longer, but his feather bed offered little respite from the discomfort of his mind. As soon as his servant brought word that Elizabeth had survived the night he had packed up and said his good-byes to his stepfather. He stared out of the window at Claegburn Woods. *This time, he would not come back.*

The day was bright and fair, a perfect day for an imperfect purpose. He cursed the blasted sunshine, wishing instead for dark thunderous clouds, wild winds, and a thrashing rain. In answer, birds twittered inanely.

The coach bumped unexpectedly and lurched to the side, skidding to a halt. A smooth road. Nothing there to break an axle on. He'd ridden down this road ten dozen times in the past weeks. What could be amiss? He peered out of the window and then closed his eyes tight, falling back against his seat, astonished. He must be dreaming, still in his bed, and this simply another fitful nightmare.

But no, he was wide awake and this was unbelievably real.

He flung the door open and charged out of the coach ready to strangle them—one and all. "This is outside of enough! Are you mad? It's broad daylight! You're bound to be seen. And who's taking care of Elizabeth?"

Bertie stood unmoved, black eye mask, absurd beard, a cocked French cap, and a rather capable looking over-and-under pointed directly at him. "Stand and deliver."

"Deliver what? Have your wits gone begging? I have no jewels. If you wanted blunt, I would gladly have obliged you without this charade."

"Quiet." She growled, and then gestured with her pistol. "Turn around. Do as I say. I'm not above putting a vent in your spleen."

"Have at it." He opened his arms wide. "I don't give a fig if you do."

From the rear of the coach, he heard a familiar old voice rasp. "Stop yammering with him and get on with it. Can't stand here all day. I've got mending to attend to." Trace turned to find Rose, in black pantaloons, a purple satin sash with eyeholes tied around her head, her hair waving wildly like a white bush, as she bound the footman's hands.

Trace shook his head in disbelief. "Heavens above, Bertie. What did you do? Bring them all?"

Lavinnia, scarcely disguised in a pirate's bandanna and mask, toddled toward him. "I don't usually come. Thought I'd better this time, what with Lizzy . . . Oh, but that's the point, isn't it?" She waggled her foil in his direction. "Come along without a fuss."

He heard light footfalls on the top of the coach. That, he suspected, must be one of the twins. Clad in black men's garb, a small figure leapt nimbly down from the top of the coach. *Bonnie.*

Bertie hissed to the girl under her breath. "Did you pay them?"

"*Oui!*" Bonnie grinned, beneath a crooked beard. "I thought we agreed to tie this one up as well."

"Mad as hatters, all of you. Reasonable human beings do not behave in this manner. Women, most of all. You're supposed to be the gentler sex—"

Nana Rose grumbled. "Get on with it. Don't feel like standing here all day listening to him prose on."

"Turn around." Bertie prodded Trace's shoulder.

What ought I do? What can I do, aside from thrashing the lot of them—widows, spinsters, and chits? Hardly the gentlemanly thing. He shook his head and turned around.

Lavinnia nudged him in the side with her foil, obviously

unaware of the sharpness of the point. "Bend down. I can't reach. I'm supposed to put this wretched sack over your head. Now there's a good lad."

A good lad. Lunatics. Am I nine? And this a parlor game? They bound his hands securely and shrouded his head in one of the highwayman's infamous black hoods.

It was a dark bumpy trip in the back of their old dogcart. He hadn't the least notion why they bothered to hide his eyes. From the turns and condition of the roads, he knew exactly where they were taking him. What he could not comprehend was their purpose.

"Do you think I don't know where we are?" When they arrived at the dower house, they led him upstairs. "Did she die? Is that it? Is this retribution? If so, I welcome it. Do your worst. I deserve to be punished for not seeing what was directly under my nose. I failed her. Failed my stepfather. Chased a phantom that didn't exist."

The dower house thieves were oddly silent. They locked him in a closet. Bound and blind. What were they planning? Did they intend to leave him here to rot? He could, without a doubt, wrestle his hands free of the ropes and kick the door down. Instead, he sagged against the wall. What did it matter? If, indeed, Lizzy had died, he may as well follow suit. Weariness settled into his soul. He closed his eyes hoping sleep would take him. However, like his fitful struggle the previous night, he found no pardon in the darkness.

Time amassed itself in indecipherable clumps. When they finally opened the door, he didn't know if it had been two days or two hours. Only his bladder marked the time, and it was full. "I need to relieve myself."

"In a moment," came the delicate reply. *Blythe.* She led him gently by the hand, and he wondered if the girl was helping him escape, or if she was merely following orders from the madwomen of the dower house.

"Where are you taking me?"

"To wash up and make ready." She loosened the hood and slid it up over his head.

The sudden rush of daylight blinded him more than the darkness had. "Make ready for what?"

Blythe untied his hands without answering. "You will find everything you need here. Your word, sir, that you won't climb out the window?"

He made no promise. He'd jolly well climb out of this madhouse if, and when, he pleased.

She shrugged and she left him standing in the small bedroom, in the welcome company of a chamber pot and a washstand.

Bertie scratched at the door before she burst in. "Excellent. You're up and about. No worse for the wear, I see."

She behaved as if nothing were amiss, as if he'd been taking a nap, and this merely a dream run amok. It was entirely possible that his coach had skidded sideways and crashed.

Perhaps, he'd hit his head, and was experiencing a convoluted delusion. He remembered wounded soldiers in their stupors, crying out at invisible dragons and fantastic monsters. A shame his infertile mind could only drum up a gaggle of barmy women.

Lavinnia ambled into the room carrying a bundle, which she plopped on the bed. "Everything is ready. Let's see if these fit."

She held a long black gown up to his shoulders. "Oh dear, he's broader than I anticipated."

Bertie snorted. "It'll do. Only for one day, after all."

"What is it for?" Trace couldn't keep the snarl out of his voice. "Burial garb?"

"Oh, good heavens, no." Lavinnia twittered. Her faded gold ringlets bounced ridiculously under her mobcap. "Although, I suppose, if you think of it, in one fashion it may well signify a death."

"Enough jabbering. Put the robe on him." Bertie reached for a lump of wadding and shook it out. "Lord Mulvern will be here shortly."

"Mulvern! Blast it all, Bertie! What does my stepfather have to do with any of this? One thing to waylay me, but if you've harmed one hair on his—"

Bertie held up her hand. "Arriving on his own accord. And I'll thank you to mind your tongue around gentlewomen, young man." She glanced pointedly at Lavinnia.

CUT FROM THE SAME CLOTH

The widow smiled graciously at him and shook out the black cloak. "Oh, never mind that. Bound to be overwrought, isn't he?"

Overwrought? He laughed sourly. *Am I overwrought, or on the verge of joining your ranks and becoming a bedlamite myself?* He allowed plump little Lavinnia to slide the garment on his arms, tug, and adjust it to fit his shoulders.

"That will suffice." Bertie prodded him forward. "Across the hall with you then."

They led him into the parlor.

"Lizzy!" *Alive. Thank God!* A part of his heart sprang back to life. At least, in all this madness, there was good news.

She sat in a peculiar enclosure, a square table turned on its side, boxing her in. Elizabeth lowered her head, averting her eyes from his, arm and shoulder bound in white bandages, her pallor ashen. *She should be in bed.*

The rest of the room had been oddly rearranged. Bertie guided him toward the far end, where a small desk sat, each of the legs propped up on a stack of books. The old Elizabethan chair Bertie was so fond of sat behind it raised up on an old woodbin.

"Sit." Bertie ordered.

He recognized the tableau then, and guessed their plan. They'd arranged the chairs to mimic a magistrate's court. Elizabeth sat in a makeshift dock. And Bertie was directing him to the judge's bench.

"I'll have no part in this." He shoved back and bumped into the wall.

Bertie folded her arms across her sagging bosom. "You will step up and do your duty, or do I have to get out my blunderbuss?"

Two could play at this intimidation game. He crossed his arms and towered over her. "You may choose whichever weapon from your arsenal you desire. *I. Won't. Do. It.*"

Lavinnia patted his arm, as if he was a small boy she could cajole into behaving properly. "You won't do *what,* dear?"

"Judge. Judge *her.* I won't."

"You already have, I'd say." Bertie muttered, while fiddling with the wadding in the wig she held.

"She's right, you know." Earnestness sat oddly on Lavinnia's normally cheery face. "The least you can do is finish the job."

Rose snarled at him from the doorway. "Unless you're a coward."

He held his roiling temper in check. "This is nonsense! If you insist on judgment, call a magistrate."

"We have. He should arrive at any moment." Bertie held up the wig as if sizing it to his head.

He glared at her, too late remembering exactly who the magistrate was.

Lavinnia smiled at him. "Naturally, we all hold our magistrate in high esteem, but do you think your step-papa would be able to send the women of his own house to Newgate?"

"Humph. I say, he would do it in a trice." Nana Rose snapped her fingers.

Lavinnia shook her head mournfully. "No. It would break the dear man's heart. It falls to you, Trace. You are the only one who can judge fairly."

"Fairly? Me? How can I possibly judge her fairly? Don't you know—"

"Yes. Are you daft? Of course, we know." Nana Rose marched toward him. "Lavinnia's idea to put you up to this. Any fool could tell you loved Lizzy. Saved the gel's life, didn't you? But you also had the backbone to turn your back on her because of her crimes."

"Don't you see?" Lavinnia asked brightly, as if it were simple mathematics, the adding of two numbers to arrive at a sum.

Only he *did not* see. This was some convoluted female logic designed to muddle a man's thinking – like Eve convincing Adam to take a bite. They surrounded him, an army of irrational females.

Bertie tried to elucidate. "Being a military man, you're the only one who wouldn't whitewash it. You go by the rules, don't you, lad?"

He frowned. They were trying to trick him. Even so, this line of reasoning tempted him too much not to refine upon it for this merry band of thieves. "Without laws, society would be intolerable. Ruthless. Anarchy. No one, *not even you, ladies,* would be safe without the rule of law."

"Exactly." Lavinnia nodded. "And yet, you didn't report our Lizzy."

His breath seemed to hang up in his neck somewhere. He glanced uncomfortably at the docks and caught Elizabeth peering attentively in his direction. She hastened to look away.

Trace didn't know what to say.

"That's how we know you're the perfect man to act as judge. *'Justice tempered with mercy.'* Mr. Milton said that." Lavinnia seemed quite pleased with herself.

"Shakespeare," Nana Rose corrected.

"Oh, no, I'm quite certain it's Mr. Milton."

"No matter." Rose waved away her daughter-in-law's protestations. "Point is, the silly girl won't eat." She nodded in Lizzy's direction. "She's lost the will to live. We can't force her to get well, now can we? This is the only way."

"Yes. We've all agreed." Lavinnia's head bobbed sagely. "After you hear our case, we'll abide by your decision, no matter what it is. We trust you'll choose the wisest course. If you think we should turn ourselves in, we will. They might hang us. But, I rather think, it would be deportation."

Bertie brightened. "Australia. Whales in that hemisphere. I wouldn't mind seeing another part of the world—"

"Bertie!" Nana Rose snapped.

"It would be a terrible burden to leave this task upon your stepfather's shoulders." Lavinnia took the old parliamentary wig from Bertie and held it up to Trace. "Will you do it? For Lizzy's sake?"

Chapter 8
Tossed Upon Cloudy Seas

TRACE TOOK THE bedraggled peruke Lavinnia offered and flopped it down on the writing desk. "No wig. If we're going to do this, we'll do it my way." He lifted the Elizabethan chair down from the makeshift dais and set it squarely on the floor. Frowning at the improvised docks imprisoning Lizzy, he started to move the inverted table away.

Lizzy put her hand on the edge. "Leave it."

"It's absurd."

"I prefer it."

He straightened and exhaled loudly. "As you wish."

A clatter in the foyer and a flurry of footsteps on the stairs alerted Trace to his stepfather's arrival.

Lord Mulvern charged into the parlor, breathless. "What's

all this then? A note arrived, saying the highwaymen had been captured."

Lavinnia scurried to his side, "It's true, my lord. Come and sit down." She led him to a chair on the right side of the room.

He continued to stand. Confusion registered on his features as he absorbed the changes in the parlor and his stepson standing in the center. "I thought you took your leave this morning."

"As did I."

"Where is he then? The French rascal?"

Trace rubbed his jaw for a moment before answering. *No sense beating about the bush.* With a wry half-smile, Trace waved his hand at the prisoner in the docks. "Allow me to introduce you to Lady Elizabeth Claegburn. Behold, my lord, *The Frenchman.*" His gesture grandly encompassed the rest of the women standing mute in the parlor. "And her band of merry thieves."

He admired the way Lizzy unflinchingly met Lord Mulvern's astonished gaze.

Mulvern shook his head. "Called me here for a jest, did you? A prank? Well, I am not amused. Ain't funny, lad." He frowned. "What happened to her arm?"

"I shot her." Trace waited for the truth to settle on his stepfather.

"Shot Lizzy? No. You wouldn't do such a thing, unless . . ." Mulvern dropped into the chair. "No. I don't believe it.

Couldn't be. Not a woman."

While Mulvern sat muttering, digesting this unsettling revelation, Bertie rang a bell. "Oyez! Oyez! This hearing is now in session."

Trace frowned at her. "I think we can dispense with the formalities."

Bertie sniffed indignantly. "It's *court*, lad. Calls for an air of authority."

He began to lose patience. "You do realize this is the only place in the civilized world where I am addressed as *lad*. *Captain*, I answer to. My mother's family, in which I am the male heir, address me as Lord Ryerton, or my lord. If you wish to lend authority to these proceedings, try something other than *lad*."

"Very well, *Your Honor*." Bertie smiled smugly. "Oyez! Oyez! Court is now in session." She rang the bell.

Lord Mulvern glanced at his female relatives, his brow pinching into a thick gray V. "What's this? Court?"

Lavinnia stood beside him and patted his arm. "Yes. We rather hoped you would represent the Crown."

"Gad, this must be a hallucination — brought on by a bad mushroom in my omelet."

Trace sat down facing them. "All too real, I'm afraid. They want to present their case to us."

Lavinnia cleared her throat. "For my first witness, I call the Dowager Countess of Mulvern, Lady Rose."

Rose sat grudgingly in the witness chair. Before anyone asked her a question, she pointed her finger at Lord Mulvern. "None of this would be happening if it weren't for you — murderer! It ought to be you sitting in the docks, instead of our Lizzy."

Mulvern slapped his hands against his knees. "How many times are you going to dredge up that old saw?"

"Till somebody listens. And I'll keep bringing it up until it's you swinging from Tyburn. And now, on account of you, our Lizzy might—"

"I've told you a hundred times, I did not kill Royce. The mere suggestion is—"

Rose thumped her fist on the chair arm. "He died directly after you went to his room."

"Of lung fever, Rose. That's why I came. To see my brother before he passed away."

"No. You hated him. You were always jealous. You wanted the title. And then when my sons died . . . You couldn't wait to turn us out of Claegburn."

"You go too far, old woman. You know full well, I offered you, *all of you,* a place in the manor." Every other female gaze in the room whipped to Rose. Mouths agape. They hadn't known. Rose had kept that tidbit from them.

Lord Mulvern rubbed his temples. "And don't think I wasn't deuced nervous about offering, too. What with you running about calling me a murderer at every turn, I half expected you'd poison m' food."

"I considered it," Rose muttered venomously under her breath.

Mulvern ignored her. "But, no. You wouldn't have any of it. Now it's come to this. If you wanted funds, you should have applied to me."

"What? Come begging to *you?*"

This tirade was going nowhere. Trace decided to put an end to it, but Lizzy beat him to it.

"Stop!" She half stood in the box, but then sagged back into her chair. "Stop. You can't blame him any longer. And above all, not for this. This was our doing. *My* doing."

Nana Rose crossed her arms defensively, but said nothing.

Lizzy rested her head on her hand. "It's so much easier to have a name, a face, to turn our anger at, Nana. Pneumonia took grandfather. And my parents' carriage wheel broke of its own accord." She glanced at the women of her family. "It's grotesquely unfair that they should be crushed, killed in that accident, and I thrown free." She shook her head. "In lieu of hating providence, it was easier for all of us to blame Lord Mulvern." She glanced at her uncle, sorrowful. "I'm sorry, my lord. This is none of your doing. This entire situation is owing to our own foolish pride."

Nana Rose stood up. "What of the tenants! That's his doing. Without us, what would've happened to the Turners, or Bernards, or . . . ? Well, you know how many of them we helped. It's all in the book. He should have been taking care of them and the estates. It's shameful how he let it run to shambles."

Lavinnia clapped her hands together, signaling a close to the discussion. "Thank you very much, Rose. Step down, please. Bonnie, dear, will you come to testify?"

Trace held up his hand, forestalling them. "What book?"

Lavinnia smiled graciously. "The accounting book, of course, your Lordship."

He glanced wildly at Lizzy. "You kept a record?"

She raised a small accounting book from her lap just high enough for him to see the deuced thing really existed.

Bonnie trudged up and took her grandmother's place in the witness chair. She pleaded with Trace straight off. "You can't blame Lizzy alone. She wanted to take Blythe and me to London for a proper season, so we wouldn't end up old maids like her and Bertie."

Old maid.

The chit didn't mince words. She may as well have plunged a knife into Trace's heart. *Lizzy thought she was an old maid.* He'd left her here alone, uncertain of her expectations. He'd ridden off to the battlefield thinking their future was obvious, a certainty. She'd concluded it was a lost dream.

He pressed his lips together and lowered his head to his hands. What a mess they'd all made of things. He stood up suddenly, and went to the prisoner's box. If only she'd look at him. He shrugged out of the black robe and tossed it aside. She still would not meet his gaze.

Even bruised and pale, her face was beautiful to him—not necessarily the lines or features, but the woman that face described. He knew then, he would have come back for her. He was a fool to have thought otherwise. She meant everything to him. He would ride into Hades if he had to. He held out his hand. "I would like to see that book, if I may?"

Lizzy lifted it up to him in shaking hands, reluctantly, like a student handing in an examination book, knowing full well the answers therein would add up to a failing grade.

He tried to relieve her trepidation. "Four years. How many coaches could you have robbed? Only a handful, surely."

By her raised brow, Trace knew he'd been optimistic. He glanced at the other women, all carefully avoiding his inspection. He returned to the dubious comfort of Bertie's chair.

"Not much else to do in this part of the empire," Bertie muttered.

Bonnie sat watching, fidgeting nervously, as he turned the pages. His heart sank lower with every carefully written ledger sheet.

Lavinnia cleared her throat. "Please bear in mind, Your Honor. We are all guilty."

"Yes, it's on all of us," Bonnie added.

"Don't listen to them," Lizzy urged, speaking at last. "It was *my* doing. They never would've fallen into it, if I hadn't. . ."

He didn't look up. He kept his eyes on the page. If he looked up now, she would know how intensely he admired her courage, how this whole thing was breaking him inside. She'd done it for them, yet she willingly took full responsibility. His jaw tightened painfully in a futile attempt to keep his emotions in check while he kept reading and tallying.

Lord Mulvern shook his head. "How bad is it, son?"

He couldn't answer yet. He had more pages to calculate. Dear God, they'd been busy in his absence.

When at last Trace closed the book, he stared thoughtfully at the ladies of the dower house. "Do you all agree to abide by my decision?"

They nodded, with varying degrees of reluctance, even Rose.

"And, Lord Mulvern, do you agree as well?"

His stepfather rubbed at his temple, as if trying to find relief from a burgeoning megrim. "The whole thing is a confounded muddle. A scandalous tangle. Women of my own house—thieves? I can't comprehend it. Most of all *you*, Lavinnia." He cast a forlorn glance at the solicitor for the defense. "I was on the point of asking you to be my . . . had hoped you might consider . . ."

Lavinnia chewed the corner of her lip, but wisely didn't interrupt.

Lord Mulvern waved his hand, as if too weary to finish

speaking his mind. "Yes. If you can sort out this muddle, Trace, then by all means, I'll stand with you."

Trace nodded. "And Lizzy? Will you submit to whatsoever punishment for your crimes I deem necessary?"

He thought it impossible that her face could turn any paler, but it did. *She was weakening. Any moment she would pass out. He must hurry.* She nodded, almost imperceptibly.

"Very well. I'm ready to state my verdict." *Ring the blessed bell,* Trace thought. But Bertie, the bell ringer, gripped the edge of her seat, as frozen as the rest of them.

"Lady Elizabeth Claegburn, I find you guilty of armed robbery against the King's subjects."

She sagged.

He wanted to gather her up in his arms and hold her, but this was a moment she must bear on her own. A moment that would alter the course of their lives. "For these crimes, which are numerous," he held up the cursed accounting book, "I order you to anonymously repay all that you have stolen."

Nana Rose jumped to her feet. "She can't! Look at her. How in heaven's name do you expect her to pay it back? It's spent. Tenants' roofs. Clothing. Food—"

Blythe stood up. "Our London fund. Take the London fund."

"Not nearly enough." Nana Rose planted her fists on her hips. "Impossible!"

"Silence." Trace held up his hand. "Sit down!" he roared.

"You asked for judgment. I'm *judging*."

He turned back to Elizabeth. "However, I offer you an alternative sentence."

"Deportation?" Bertie asked.

He held up a silencing finger, before returning to his pale prisoner. "I will pay your debt."

"No." Lizzy looked up at him, startled. "I couldn't. It's not your debt. You shouldn't have to pay for my—"

"No, lad. She's right. Not your debt." Lord Mulvern stood and protested vigorously. "They gave the money to my tenants. Rose has the right of it. It should've fallen to me, anyway."

"A portion, perhaps. However, you, Lord Mulvern, will be held responsible for attending to your tenants' future with far more diligence. We will discuss that at length later. At the moment, Lady Elizabeth *must answer* her sentence."

Trace focused on Lizzy. "As your husband, your debt would become mine. I will pay it off immediately."

"As my . . . ?"

"Yes. I'm offering a lifetime sentence, not as a criminal, but as my wife. During which time, I believe you will be legally bound to love, honor, cajole, play chess, kiss, raise children, and did I mention love?" He was certain he had.

Lizzy swallowed hard. Her eyes shimmered with impending tears. Trace feared what he saw there: remorse, shame, and reticence. *She was going to refuse him.* He shook his head. "Oh, Lizzy, don't say no. I beg you. I'm going to pay it off anyway, and gladly. Only say you'll have me? Say it!"

She covered her mouth with her fingers, to hide her quivering lips. He waited for her answer. A thousand hopes bloomed and died and sprouted anew before she managed a choke out a reply. "But you said you couldn't love a thief."

The heavy dark lifted its iron lid from his heart, and he felt it beat once again. "Evidently, I was wrong."

She smiled then, and nodded, radiant as an angel under a waterfall of tears.

Good thing he knew what that nod meant. He yanked away the annoying prisoner's box and scooped her up into his arms. "Yes," she whispered into his neck. "Yes."

He kissed her, his sweet Lizzy, to the accompaniment of the elder women sighing, and younger women *oh*-ing.

"And now, my love, it's time you rested." He carried her away from the courtroom and off to her bedroom.

He laid her down on the bed, the dark stain of blood from the previous night gone and fresh white linen in its place. He sat down beside her, smoothing strands of midnight black hair back from her wet cheeks. Her color looked better already.

He could not resist kissing her once more. "No more tears, Lizzy, my sweet. Rest. Gather your strength. You have a long and tedious sentence ahead of you. A lifetime of loving me will not be easy. Years and years of kisses whenever I demand them, which I suspect will be often. And then there's . . . " He grinned at her speculatively.

She laughed, and with her good arm pulled him down to her eager mouth.

He smiled into her greedy kiss. *Perhaps not so tedious after all.*

෨ ඞ

Dear Reader,

I hope you enjoyed *The Highwayman Came Waltzing*. I've always loved Alfred Noyes's poem. A copy of it follows directly after this letter. Keep turning the pages for an excerpt from my new series, The Stranje House Novels. More Regency fun, but this time with some unusual young ladies who are learning to be spies in the Napoleonic wars.

If you would like to learn more about the realities of highwaymen versus myth and legend, visit my website. You'll find it on my blog, or follow the Historical Extras link on my Bookclub page.

KathleenBaldwin.com

If you would like contests, story extras, or you want to be first to hear when my next book is coming out, sign up for Kathleen's Newsletter. Your email will be kept private, and I only send out a newsletter a few times a year.

Meanwhile, happy reading,

Kathleen Baldwin

IF YOU ENJOYED READING THIS BOOK, please **lend** your copy to a friend, ***recommend*** it to your book club, or ***write a review!*** Your reviews help other readers discover your favorite books.

The Highwayman
By Alfred Noyes

PART ONE

The wind was a torrent of darkness among the gusty trees.
The moon was a ghostly galleon tossed upon cloudy seas.
The road was a ribbon of moonlight over the purple moor,
And the highwayman came riding—
Riding—riding—
The highwayman came riding, up to the old inn-door.

He'd a French cocked hat on his forehead, a bunch of lace at his chin,
A coat of the claret velvet, and breeches of brown doeskin.
They fitted with never a wrinkle. His boots were up to the thigh.
And he rode with a jeweled twinkle,
His pistol butts a-twinkle,
His rapier hilt a-twinkle, under the jeweled sky.

Over the cobbles he clattered and clashed in the dark inn-yard.
He tapped with his whip on the shutters, but all was locked and barred.
He whistled a tune to the window, and who should be waiting there
But the landlord's black-eyed daughter,
Bess, the landlord's daughter,
Plaiting a dark red love-knot into her long black hair.

And dark in the dark old inn-yard a stable-wicket creaked
Where Tim the ostler listened. His face was white and peaked.

His eyes were hollows of madness, his hair like mouldy hay,
But he loved the landlord's daughter,
The landlord's red-lipped daughter.
Dumb as a dog he listened, and he heard the robber say—

"One kiss, my bonny sweetheart, I'm after a prize to-night,
But I shall be back with the yellow gold before the morning light;
Yet, if they press me sharply, and harry me through the day,
Then look for me by moonlight,
Watch for me by moonlight,
I'll come to thee by moonlight, though hell should bar the way."

He rose upright in the stirrups. He scarce could reach her hand,
But she loosened her hair in the casement. His face burnt like a brand
As the black cascade of perfume came tumbling over his breast;
And he kissed its waves in the moonlight,
(O, sweet black waves in the moonlight!)
Then he tugged at his rein in the moonlight, and galloped away to the west.

PART TWO

He did not come in the dawning. He did not come at noon;
And out of the tawny sunset, before the rise of the moon,
When the road was a gypsy's ribbon, looping the purple moor,
A red-coat troop came marching—
Marching—marching—
King George's men came marching, up to the old inn-door.

They said no word to the landlord. They drank his ale instead.

But they gagged his daughter, and bound her, to the foot of her narrow bed.

Two of them knelt at her casement, with muskets at their side!

There was death at every window;

And hell at one dark window;

For Bess could see, through her casement, the road that *he* would ride.

They had tied her up to attention, with many a sniggering jest.

They had bound a musket beside her, with the muzzle beneath her breast!

"Now, keep good watch!" and they kissed her. She heard the doomed man say—

Look for me by moonlight;

Watch for me by moonlight;

I'll come to thee by moonlight, though hell should bar the way!

She twisted her hands behind her; but all the knots held good!

She writhed her hands till her fingers were wet with sweat or blood!

They stretched and strained in the darkness, and the hours crawled by like years

Till, now, on the stroke of midnight,

Cold, on the stroke of midnight,

The tip of one finger touched it! The trigger at least was hers!

The tip of one finger touched it. She strove no more for the rest.

Up, she stood up to attention, with the muzzle beneath her breast.

She would not risk their hearing; she would not strive again;
For the road lay bare in the moonlight;
Blank and bare in the moonlight;
And the blood of her veins, in the moonlight, throbbed to her love's refrain.

Tlot-tlot; tlot-tlot! Had they heard it? The horse hoofs ringing clear;
Tlot-tlot; tlot-tlot, in the distance? Were they deaf that they did not hear?
Down the ribbon of moonlight, over the brow of the hill,
The highwayman came riding—
  Riding—riding—
The red coats looked to their priming! She stood up, straight and still.

Tlot-tlot, in the frosty silence! *Tlot-tlot,* in the echoing night!
Nearer he came and nearer. Her face was like a light.
Her eyes grew wide for a moment; she drew one last deep breath,
Then her finger moved in the moonlight,
Her musket shattered the moonlight,
Shattered her breast in the moonlight and warned him—with her death.

He turned. He spurred to the west; he did not know who stood
Bowed, with her head o'er the musket, drenched with her own blood!
Not till the dawn he heard it, and his face grew grey to hear
How Bess, the landlord's daughter,
The landlord's black-eyed daughter,
Had watched for her love in the moonlight, and died in the darkness there.

Back, he spurred like a madman, shouting a curse to the sky,
With the white road smoking behind him and his rapier brandished high.
Blood red were his spurs in the golden noon; wine-red was his velvet coat;
When they shot him down on the highway,
Down like a dog on the highway,
And he lay in his blood on the highway, with a bunch of lace at his throat.

And still of a winter's night, they say, when the wind is in the trees,
When the moon is a ghostly galleon tossed upon cloudy seas,
When the road is a ribbon of moonlight over the purple moor,
A highwayman comes riding—
Riding—riding—
A highwayman comes riding, up to the old inn-door.

Over the cobbles he clatters and clangs in the dark inn-yard.
He taps with his whip on the shutters, but all is locked and barred.
He whistles a tune to the window, and who should be waiting there
But the landlord's black-eyed daughter,
Bess, the landlord's daughter,
Plaiting a dark red love-knot into her long black hair.

හ ෬

HERE'S A PREVIEW OF KATHLEEN'S NEW SERIES...

Award-winning YA Historical Romance from TorTeen:

"A completely original—and totally engrossing—world, full of smart girls, handsome boys, and sinister mysteries... Sign me up."
—Meg Cabot, author of *The Princess Diaries*

A School for Unusual Girls

Kathleen Baldwin

A STRANJE HOUSE NOVEL

#1 *New York Times* bestselling author Meg Cabot calls this romantic Regency adventure "completely original and totally engrossing."

New York Times Sunday Book Review calls A School for Unusual Girls, "enticing from the first sentence..."

It's 1814. Napoleon is exiled on Elba. Europe is in shambles. Britain is at war on four fronts. And Stranje House, a School for Unusual Girls, has become one of Regency England's dark little secrets. The daughters of the *beau monde* who don't fit high society's constrictive mold are banished to Stranje House to be reformed into marriageable young ladies. Or so their parents think. In truth, Headmistress Emma Stranje, the original unusual girl, has plans for the young ladies—plans that entangle the girls in the dangerous world of spies, diplomacy, and war.

After accidentally setting her father's stables on fire while performing a scientific experiment, Miss Georgiana Fitzwilliam is sent to Stranje House. But Georgie has no intention of being turned into a simpering, pudding-headed, marriageable miss. She plans to escape as soon as possible—until she meets Lord Sebastian Wyatt. Thrust together in a desperate mission to invent a new invisible ink for the English war effort, Georgie and Sebastian must find a way to work together without losing their heads—or their hearts...

Ready for a preview of the opening chapter? ⇨

#1 New York Times bestselling author **Meg Cabot** calls this romantic Regency adventure, *"completely original and totally engrossing."*

A
SCHOOL
FOR
UNUSUAL
GIRLS

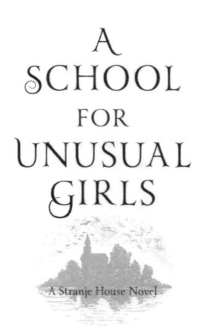

A Stranje House Novel

KATHLEEN BALDWIN

TOR®
TEEN

A TOM DOHERTY ASSOCIATES BOOK
New York

UNEDITED EXCERPT

One

BANISHED

~London, April 17, 1814~

W hat if Sir Isaac Newton's parents had packed him off to a school to reform his manners?" I smoothed my traveling skirts and risked a glance at my parents. They sat across from me, stone-faced and icy as the millpond in winter. Father did not so much as blink in my direction. But then, he seldom did. I tried again. "And if the rumors are true, not just any school—a prison."

"Do be quiet, Georgiana." With fingers gloved in mourning black, my mother massaged her forehead.

Our coach slowed and rolled to a complete standstill, waylaid by crowds spilling into Bishopsgate Street. All of London celebrated Napoleon's abdication of the French throne and his imprisonment on the isle of Elba. Rich and poor danced in the streets, raising tankards of ale, belting out military songs, roasting bread and cheese over makeshift fires. Each loud toast, every bellowed stanza, even the smell of feasting sickened me and reopened wounds of grief for the brother I'd lost two years ago in this wretched war. Their jubilation made my journey into exile all the more dismal.

Father cursed our snail-like progress through town and drummed impatient fingers against his thigh. We'd been traveling from our estate in Middlesex, north of London, since early morning. Mother closed her eyes as if in slumber, a ploy to evade my petitions. She couldn't possibly be sleeping, not while holding her spine in such an erect fashion. She refused herself the luxury of leaning back against the seat for fear of crumpling the feathers on her bonnet.

Somehow, some way, I had to convince them to turn back. "You do realize this journey is a needless expense. I have no more use for a schoolroom. I'm sixteen, and since I have already been out in society—"

Mother snapped to attention. "Oh, yes, Georgiana, I'm well aware of the fact that you have already been out in society. Indeed, I shall never forget Lady Frampton's card party."

I sighed, knowing exactly what she would say next.

"You cheated."

"I didn't. It was a simple matter of mathematics," I explained for the fortieth time. "I merely kept track of the number of cards played in each suit. How else did you expect me to win?"

"I did not *expect* you to win," she said in clipped tones. The feathers on her bonnet quivered as she clenched her jaw before continuing. "I expected you to behave like a proper young lady, not a seasoned gambler."

"Counting cards isn't considered cheating," I said quietly.

"It is when you win at every hand." She glared at me and even in the dim light of the carriage I noted a rise in her color. "And now, given your latest debacle—" She stopped. Her gaze flicked sideways to my father, gauging his expression. I would've thought it impossible for him to turn any stonier, but he did. Her voice knotted so tight she practically hissed, "I doubt I shall *ever* be allowed to show my face in Lady Frampton's company again, or for that matter in polite society *anywhere*."

Trumped. She'd slapped down the Queen of Ruination card, *Georgiana Fitzwilliam, the destroyer*. I drew back the curtain and stared out the window. A man with a drunken grin tipped his hat and waved a gin bottle, as if inviting us to join the celebration. He tugged a charwoman into a riotous jig and twirled away.

Lucky fellow.

"Bothersome peasants." My mother huffed and adjusted the cuff of her traveling coat. *Peasant* was her favorite condemnation. She followed it with a haughty sniff, as if breathing *peasant* air made her nose itch. A roar of laughter rocked the crowd outside entertained by a man on stilts dressed as General Wellington kicking a straw dummy of Napoleon.

"Confound it." Father grumbled and consulted his pocket watch. "At this pace we won't get there 'til dark. All this ruckus over that pompous little Corsican. *Fools.* Anyone with any sense knows Bonaparte was done for a month ago."

Without weighing the consequences, I spoke my fears aloud. "One can never be certain with Napoleon, can they? He may have abdicated the throne, but he kept his title."

"*Emperor.* Bah! Devil take him. Emperor of what? The sticks and stones on Elba." Father bristled and puffed up as if he might explode. "General Wellington should've shot the blighter when he had the chance. Bonaparte is too arrogant by half. The man doesn't know when to give up. Let that be a lesson to you, Georgie." He shook a finger at me as if I were in league with the infamous Emperor. "Know when to give up, young lady. If you did, we wouldn't be stuck here in the middle of all this rabble waiting to get across London Bridge."

Never mind that during the last ten years Napoleon Bonaparte had embroiled all of Europe in a terrible war—today I was the villain.

But I forgave my father's burst of temper and heartily wished I'd kept my mouth shut. His anger was understandable. My brother Robert died in a skirmish with Napoleon's troops shortly before the Battle of Salamanca. Reminders of the war surrounded us. Perhaps if we had been the ones burning Napoleon in effigy it would have been liberating. Although it had been more than two years, each redcoat soldier who sauntered past, each raucous guffaw jarred our coach as if we'd been blasted by the same cannonball that killed Robbie.

My father would never admit to a weakness such as grief. I didn't have that luxury. Gravity could not explain the weight that crushed my chest whenever I thought of Robbie's death. He had been the best and kindest of my brothers. We were closest in age. I hardly knew my two oldest brothers; they'd been away at Cambridge and had no interest in making my acquaintance. Robbie, alone, had genuinely liked me. He never looked at me as if I was an ugly mouse that had crawled out from under the rug. I missed how he would scruff my unruly red hair and challenge me to a chess game, or tell me about books he'd read, or places he'd visited.

Napoleon stole him from us.

If we'd been home, Father would've stomped out of the house and gone hunting with his beloved hounds. Some hapless hare would've paid the price of his wrath. Instead, this laborious journey to haul me off to Stranje House kept him pinned up with painful reminders. Unfortunately, Napoleon wasn't present to shoulder his share of the blame. Father furrowed his great hairy eyebrows at me, the troublesome runt in his litter.

If only I'd had the good grace to be born a boy. *What use is a daughter?* How many times had I heard him ask this? And answer. *Useless baggage.* Three sons had been sufficient. Even after Robbie's death, Father still had his heir and a spare. I was simply a nuisance, a miscalculation.

The leather seats creaked as I shifted under his condemning frown. He'd never bestowed upon me more than a passing interest. Until now. Now, I'd finally done something to merit his attention. Not as I'd hoped, not as I'd wished, but I had finally won his notice. He squinted at me as if I was the cause of all this uproar.

I swallowed hard. "We could turn back and make the journey another day."

My father growled in response and thumped the ceiling with his walking stick alerting our coachman. "Blast it all, man! Get this rig rolling."

"Make way," the coachman shouted at the throng and cracked his whip. Our coach lumbered slowly forward. With each turn of the wheel, my hope of a reprieve sank lower and lower. Before we crossed the bridge, I took one last look at the crowds milling on boardwalks and cobblestones, reveling and jostling one another. One last glimpse of freedom as I sat confined in gloomy silence on my way to be imprisoned at Stranje House and beaten into submission.

With a weary huff my mother exhaled. "For heaven's sake, Georgiana, stop gawking at the rabble and sit up like a proper young lady."

I straightened, prepared to sit this way forever if she would reconsider. She sniffed and pretended to sleep again.

We passed the outskirts of London with the sun high above us, a dull brass coin unable to burn through the thick haze of coal soot and smoke that hung over the city. We traveled the south for hours, stopping only once at a posting inn in Tunbridge Wells to change the horses and eat. As evening approached, the sky turned a mournful gray and the faded pink horizon reminded me of dead roses. Except for Father's occasional snoring, we traveled in stiff, suffocating silence. Two hours past nightfall, we turned off the macadam road onto a bumpy gravel drive and stopped.

Sliding down the window glass, I leaned out to have a closer look and inhaled the sharp salty tang of sea air. The coachman clambered down and opened a creaking iron gate. A rusty placard proclaimed the old manor as STRANJE HOUSE, but I knew better. This wasn't a house. Or a school.

This was to be my cage.

"It must be well after eight. Surely, it's too late to impose upon them tonight. We could stop at an inn and come back tomorrow."

Father hoisted his jaw to an implacable angle. "No. Best to get it over and done with tonight."

"The headmistress is expecting us." Mother straightened her bonnet and sat with even greater dignity.

Our coachman coaxed the team through the entrance and clanged the gate shut behind us. The horses shied at the sound of barking in the distance, not normal barking—howls and yips. Seconds later, dogs raced from the shadows. It might have been two, two dozen, or two hundred. Impossible to tell. They seemed to be everywhere at once, silent except for their ferocious breathing. One of them pounced at the coachman's boot as he scrambled to his perch.

I jerked back from my window as one of the creatures leaped up against the coach door. Black as night, except for yellow eyes and moon-white teeth, the monstrous animal peered in at me as if curious. I couldn't breathe, couldn't move, could do naught but stare back. Our coachman swore, cracked his whip, and the horses sprang forward. The beast's massive paws slipped from my window. With a sharp yip, he fell away from the coach. These were no ordinary dogs.

"Wolves." I slammed the window glass up and secured the latch.

"Nonsense," my mother said, but scooted farther from the door. "Everyone knows there are no more wolves in England. They were all killed off during King Henry's reign."

"Might've missed one or two," my father muttered, peering out his window at our shadowy entourage.

Whatever they were, these black demons would devour us the minute we stepped out of the coach. "Turn back. Please. I don't need this school." I hated the fear creeping into my voice.

Mother laced her fingers primly in her lap and glanced away. I cast my pride to the wind and bleated like a lamb before slaughter. "I'll do exactly as you ask. I promise. Best manners. Everything. I'll even intentionally lose at cards. I give you my word."

They paid me no heed.

Stranje House loomed larger by the second. Our coach bumped along faster than it had all day, the coachman ran the team full out in an effort to outpace the wolves. My heart galloped along with the horses. Faster and faster we rumbled up the drive, until the speed of it made me sick to my stomach.

The sprawling Elizabethan manor crouched on scraggily

unkempt grounds. Dead trees stood among the living, stripped of bark by the salt air they stretched white skeletal hands toward the dark sky. The roof formed a black silhouette against the waning moonlight. Sharp peaks jutted up like jagged scales on a dragon's back. Fog and mist blew up from the sea and swirled around the boney beast.

Gripping the seat, I turned to my parents. "You can't mean to leave me in this decrepit old mausoleum? You can't." They refused to meet my frantic gaze. "Father?"

"Hound's tooth, Georgie! Leave off."

My heart banged against my ribs like a trapped bat. No reprieve. No pardon. No mercy.

Where could I turn for help? If Robbie were alive, he wouldn't let them do this. My stuffy older brothers would applaud locking me away. Geoffrey, the oldest, had written to say, "She's an embarrassment to the family. About time she was taught some manners." I doubt Edward remembers I even exist. Thus, I would be banished to this bleak heap of stones, this monstrous cage surrounded by hellhounds.

All too soon, the coach rolled to a stop in front of the dragon's dark gaping mouth. I couldn't breathe. I wanted to scream, to shriek like a cat being thrown into a river to drown.

Only I didn't. I sank back against the seat and gasped for air.

From my window, I watched as an elderly butler with all the warmth of a grave digger emerged from the house and issued a sharp staccato whistle. The wolves immediately took off and ran to the trees at the edge of the old house. But I saw them pacing, watching us hungrily from the shadows.

To my dismay, our coach door opened and a footman lowered the steps. I hung back as long as possible. My parents were almost to the house when, on wobbly legs, I climbed out and followed them inside, past the grizzled butler, and up a wooden staircase. Every step carried me further from my home, further from freedom. Each riser seemed taller than the last, harder to climb, and my feet heavier, until at last the silent butler ushered us into the headmistress's cramped, dimly lit study.

We sat before her enormous desk on small uncomfortable chairs, my parents in the forefront, me in the back. Towering bookshelves lined the walls. More books sat in haphazard piles on the floor, stacked like druid burial stones.

Concentrating on anything, except my fate, I focused on the titles of books piled nearest my chair. A translation of *Beowulf* lay atop a collection of John Donne's sermons, a human anatomy book, and Lord Byron's scandalous vampire tale, *The Giaour*. A most unsettling assortment. I stopped reading and could scarcely keep from biting my lip to the point of drawing blood.

The headmistress, Miss Emma Stranje, sat behind her desk, mute, assessing me with unsettling hawk eyes. In the flickering light of the oil lamp, I couldn't tell her age. She looked youthful one minute, and ancient the next. She might've been pretty once, if it weren't for her shrewd measuring expression. She'd pulled her wavy brown hair back into a severe chignon knot, but stray wisps escaped their moorings giving her a feral catlike appearance.

I tried not to cower under her predatory gaze. If this woman intended to be my jailer, I needed to stand my ground now or I would never fight my way out from under her thumb.

My mother cleared her throat and started in, "You know why we are here. As we explained in our letters—"

"It was an accident!" I blurted, and immediately regretted it. The words sounded defensive, not strong and reasoned as I had intended.

Mother pinched her lips and sat perfectly straight, primly picking lint off her gloves as if my outburst caused the bothersome flecks to appear. She sighed. I could almost hear her oft repeated complaint, *"Why is Georgiana not the meek biddable daughter I deserve?"*

Miss Stranje arched one imperious eyebrow, silently demanding the rest of the explanation, waiting, unnerving me with every tick of the clock. My mind turned to mush. How much explanation should I give? If I told her the plain truth she'd know too much about my unacceptable pursuits. If I said too little I'd sound like an arsonist. In the ensuing silence, she tapped one slender finger against the dark walnut of her desk. The sound echoed through the room—a magistrate's gavel, consigning me to life in her prison. "You *accidentally* set fire to your father's stables?"

My father growled low in his throat and shifted angrily on the delicate Hepplewhite chair.

"Yes," I mumbled, knowing the fire wasn't the whole reason I was here, merely the final straw, a razor-sharp spearlike straw. Unfortunately, there were several dozen pointy spears in my parents' quiver of *what's-wrong-with-Georgiana.*

If only they understood. If only the world cared about something beyond my ability to pour tea and walk with a mincing step. I decided to tell Miss Stranje at least part of the truth. "It was a scientific experiment gone awry. Had I been successful—"

"Successful?" roared my father. He twisted on the flimsy chair, putting considerable stress on the rear legs as he leaned in my direction, numbering my sins on his fingers. "You nearly roasted my prize hunters alive! Every last horse—scared senseless. Burned the bleedin' stables to the ground. *To the ground!* Nothing left but a heap of charred stone. Our house and fields would've gone up next if the tenants and neighbors hadn't come running to help. That ruddy blaze would've taken their homes and crops, too. *Successful?* You almost reduced half of High Cross Greene to ash."

Every word a lashing, I nodded and kept my face to the floor, knowing he wasn't done.

"As it was, you scorched more than half of Squire Thurgood's apple orchard. I'll be paying dearly for those lost apples over the next three years, I can tell you that. And what about my hounds!" He paused for breath and clamped his teeth together so tight that veins bulged at his temples and his whole head trembled with repressed rage.

In that short fitful silence, I could not help but remember the sound of those dogs baying and whimpering, and the faces of our servants and neighbors smeared with ash as we all struggled to contain the fire, their expressions—grim, angry, wishing me to perdition.

"My kennels are ruined. Blacker and smokier than Satan's chimney . . ." He lowered his voice, no longer clarifying for Miss Stranje's sake, and spit one final damning indictment into my face. "You almost killed my hounds!" He dismissed me with an angry wave of his hand. "Successful. Bah!"

My stomach churned and twisted with regret. *Accident.* It *was* an accident. I wished he had slapped me. It would've stung less than his disgust.

I wanted to point out the merits of inventing a new kind of undetectable invisible ink. If such an ink had been available, my brother might still be alive. As it was, the French intercepted a British courier and Robert's company found themselves caught in an ambush. It wouldn't help to say it. I tried the day after the fire and Father only got angrier. He'd shouted obscenities, called me a foolish girl. "It's done. Over. He's gone."

Nor would it help to remind him that I'd nearly died leading the horses out of the mews. His mind was made up. Unlike my father's precious livestock, my goose was well and truly cooked. He intended to banish me, imprison me here at Stranje House just as Napoleon was banished to Elba.

Miss Stranje glanced down at my mother's letter. "It says here, that on another occasion Georgiana jumped out of an attic window?"

"I didn't jump. Not exactly."

"She did." Father crossed his arms.

It had happened two and a half years ago. One would've thought they'd have forgotten it by now. "Another experiment," I admitted. "I'd read a treatise about Da Vinci and his—"

"*Wings.*" My mother cut me off and rolled her eyes upward to contemplate the ceiling. She employed the same mocking tone she always used when referring to that particular incident.

"Not wings," I defended, my voice a bit too high-pitched. "A glider. A kite."

Mother ignored me and stated her case to Miss Stranje without any inflection whatsoever. "She's a menace. Dangerous to herself and others."

"I took precautions." I forced my voice into a calmer, less ear-bruising range, and tried to explain. "I had the stable lads position a wagon of hay beneath the window."

"Yes!" Father clapped his hands together as if he'd caught a fly in them. "But you missed the infernal wagon, didn't you?"

"Because the experiment worked."

"Hardly." With a scornful grunt he explained to Miss Stranje,

"Crashed into a sycamore tree. Wore her arm in a sling for months."

"Yes, but if I'd made the kite wider and taken off from the roof—"

"This is all your doing." My father shot a familiar barb at my mother. "You never should've allowed her to read all that scientific nonsense."

"I had nothing to do with it," she bristled. "That bluestocking governess is to blame."

Miss Grissmore. An excellent tutor. A woman of outstanding patience, the only governess in ten years able to endure my incessant questions, sent packing because of my foolhardy leap. I glared at my mother's back remembering how I'd begged and explained over and over that Miss Grissmore had nothing to do with it.

"I let the woman go as soon as I realized what she was." Mother ignored Father's grumbled commentary on bluestockings and demanded of Miss Stranje, "Well? Can you reform Georgiana or not?"

There are whispers among my mother's friends that, for a large enough sum, the mysterious Miss Stranje is able to take difficult young women and mold them into marriageable misses. Her methods, however, are highly questionable. According to the gossip, Miss Stranje relies upon harsh beatings and cruel punishments to accomplish her task. Even so, ambitious parents desperate to reform their daughters turn a blind eye and even pay handsomely for her grim services. It's rumored that she even resorts to torture to transform her troublesome students into unexceptional young ladies.

Unexceptional.

Among the *beau monde,* being declared *un*exceptional by the patronesses of society is the ultimate praise. It is almost a prerequisite for marriage. Husbands do not want odd ducks like me. Being exceptional is a curse. A curse I bear.

I care less than a fig for society's good opinion. Furthermore, I haven't the slightest desire to attend their boring balls, nor do I want to stand around at a rout, or squeeze into an overcrowded sweltering soiree. More to the point, I have no intention of marrying anyone.

Ever.

My mother, on the other hand, languishes over the fact that, despite being a wealthy wool merchant's daughter with a large dowry, and having been educated in the finer arts of polite conversations, playing the pianoforte, and painting landscapes in pale watercolors, she had failed to bag herself a title. She'd married my father because he stood second in line to the Earl of Pynderham. Unfortunately, his older brother married shortly thereafter and produced several sturdy sons, thus dashing forever my mother's hopes of becoming a countess. As a result, her desire to elevate her standing in society now depends on puffing me off in marriage to an earl, or perhaps a viscount, thereby transforming her into the exalted role of mother to a countess.

A thoroughly ridiculous notion.

Has she not looked at me? My figure is flat and straight. I doubt I shall ever acquire much of a bosom. I have stubborn freckles that will not bleach out no matter how many milk baths or cucumber plasters Mother applies. She detests my ginger hair. Red is definitely not *en vogue*.

Not long after the glider incident, she tried to disguise my embarrassing red curls by rinsing them with walnut stain. It would infuriate her if she knew that her efforts to change my hair color increased my obsession with dyes and inks. Her oily walnut stain

CUT FROM THE SAME CLOTH

failed miserably. The hideous results had to be cut off—my hair shorn like a sheep. It has only now grown out to an acceptable length.

And now this. Exile to Stranje House.

I clinched the fabric of my traveling dress and wished for the millionth time that I'd been more careful while adding saltpeter to the boiling ink emulsion. If only it hadn't sparked that abominable fire.

Miss Stranje allowed an inordinate amount of time to pass before pronouncing judgment upon me.

"I knew it." Mother collapsed against the back of her chair in defeat and threw up her hands. "It's hopeless. Nothing can be done with her."

Miss Stranje rose. The black bombazine of her skirts rustled like funeral crepe. "On the contrary, Mrs. Fitzwilliam. I believe we may be able to salvage your daughter."

Salvage? They spoke of me as if I were a tattered curtain they intended to rework into a potato sack.

"You do?" My mother blinked at this astonishing news.

"Yes. However"—Miss Stranje grasped the edge of her desk as if it were a pulpit and she about to preach a sermon condemning us all to perdition—"you may have heard my teaching methods are rather unconventional. Severe. Harsh." She paused and fixed each of us with a shockingly hard glare. "I assure you, the gossip is all true."

For the first time that day, my mother relaxed.

I, on the other hand, could not swallow the dry lump of dread rising in my throat. Miss Stranje's sharp-eyed gaze seemed to reach into my soul and wring it out.

She bore down on my father. "Mr. Fitzwilliam, you may leave

133

your daughter with me under one condition. You must grant me authority in all matters pertaining to her welfare, financially and otherwise. Should I decide to lock her in a closet with only bread and water for sustenance, I will not tolerate any complaints or—"

"Heavens, no. You can't do that." Mother swished her hand through the air as if swatting away the idea. "It won't work. Don't you think we would've tried something so simple? It's no use. You can't leave her in solitude to think. She'll simply concoct more mischief while she's locked up. You'll have to come up with something more inventive than that."

Lips pressed thin, Miss Stranje sniffed. I wasn't sure whether she was annoyed about Mother interrupting or about being saddled with such an intractable student. "Furthermore," she said with a steady calm, "if I deem it necessary to take her to London to practice her social skills, you will not only permit such an excursion, you will finance the endeavor."

"More coin?" My father ran a finger around the top of his starched collar. "Already costing me a King's ransom."

"The choice is yours." She plopped a sheaf of papers on the corner of the desk nearest him. "You must sign this agreement or I will not accept your daughter into the school."

He glanced at me and his angry scowl returned. His nostrils flared. I groaned, knowing the smell of ash and burnt hay still lingered in his nose. He would sign.

"Won't sign unless I have some assurances you can do the job." He sat back, arms crossed. "We stated quite clearly in our letters, we expect some kind of guarantee. I'm no stranger to the rod. Went to Eton. Got beat regularly. All part of the training."

The lump in my stomach turned into a cannonball, and my backside began to hurt in anticipation.

"Women are too weak for this sort of thing." He glared sideways at my mother. "How do I know a female like yourself can administer proper punishment, when punishment is due?"

Miss Stranje got all prickly and tall. She didn't look weak to me. Not by half.

"I assure you, sir, although I always abide by the law and never use a rod that is thicker than my thumb—"

"Proof, Miss Stranje." Father leaned forward and tapped the stack of papers. "I want proof that you can make something of her. Then I'll sign your blasted papers."

Miss Stranje tilted her head and studied him, the way a wild turkey does before it tries to peck your eyes out. In the end, the headmistress stepped back and lifted the oil lamp. "As you wish. I believe a visit to my discipline chamber is in order." She ushered us to the door. "You, too, Georgiana, come along."

She led us down long twisting stairs, deep into the bowels of Stranje House. Damp limestone walls, gray with age and mold, closed around us, swallowing us in chilly darkness. Deeper and deeper we went. It was the hellish kind of cold, a moist heavy chill, as if the underbelly of the house had been cold for so long it had seeped into the stones permanently. It sucked the warmth straight out of my bones. We emerged in a dank hallway and shuffled through the musty passageway until the headmistress finally stopped in front of a heavy wooden door. The hinges creaked as she opened it, and we were met with the sound of human whimpering.

Miss Stranje swept her hand forward, welcoming my parents into her dungeon just as if it were a prettily decorated parlor.

Mother marched straight in, glanced about the room and shook her head. "I'm afraid there's not much here we haven't seen before." She pointed to a pale white-haired girl who was strapped waist, shoulders, and head to a thick oak slat. "See here, Henry, this is a common backboard. Very good for the posture. They had one at my finishing school. I daresay every lady in the *ton* has spent time in a similar device."

The girl's blue eyes opened wide and flittered fearfully as we drew close. Her forehead had been buckled so tightly to the backboard that red marks welted on each side of the leather strap. She stood perfectly still as Miss Stranje addressed her. "Mr. and Mrs. Fitzwilliam may I present Miss Seraphina Wyndham."

Seraphina did not speak, nor did she greet us with a genial smile. She simply mewed like a strangled kitten.

Next to Seraphina stood a large steel mummy case. I'd read about Egyptian artifacts but had never seen one. Except I quickly realized the coffin was not from ancient Egypt, not with that type of a clasp. I leaned closer, thinking I heard something inside.

Breathing.

I jumped back. "Something's in there."

"Someone," Miss Stranje corrected. Holding her lamp aloft, she peered into one of the eyeholes. The metal coffin reverberated like a dull bell when she rapped on the front. "Lady Jane? Are you—"

A sharp yowl echoed inside the metal sarcophagus.

"No need to move about. Those tines are extremely sharp. I only meant to inquire after your health. I couldn't help but notice a small quantity of blood seeping out of the bottom of the case. Are you well?"

Of course, she wasn't well. Blood trickled out of the metal seams onto the floor. "This is barbaric!" I backed away from the horrid mummy case and the even more horrid Miss Stranje.

"Well enough." Lady Jane's surly response reverberated eerily from the casket.

"Well enough, *thank you,*" Miss Stranje corrected. "One must be courteous regardless of the situation."

There was no answer.

"This is cruel." I glared at the headmistress. "You can't do this to a member of the nobility."

"Can't I?" She cocked her head at me, quizzically, like a raven right before snapping up a beetle.

A small Oriental woman padded silently out of the shadows and whacked the mummy case several times with a bamboo stick, setting off a sickening chime. I flinched as Lady Jane shrieked in pain and then obediently responded, "Well enough, *thank you.*"

My mother's only comment was, "Well now, that *is* something I haven't seen before."

Miss Stranje inclined her head to the Chinese woman and turned to my parents. "Mr. Fitzwilliam, Mrs. Fitzwilliam, allow me to present Madame Cho. She assists me here in the discipline room and also instructs the girls in Asian history."

Small and old, Madame Cho looked crafty as a black cat. She bowed slowly and stiffly as if the effort cost her ancient bones much pain.

My parents walked on without acknowledging her, following Miss Stranje to examine a rack of various sized training rods and lashes.

Swift as a thief, Madam Cho straightened. *So much for her old bones.* Her obsidian eyes reminded me of a lizard's as she examined me with ruthless assessment. I edged away and joined my father who stood toying with the end of a whip that hung on the wall. He fingered the knots tied in the leather thongs at the beating end of the whip. Glancing sideways at me, I wondered if he might be troubled by the idea of my back, lashed and bleeding.

"*Father?*" I whispered, praying for a reprieve.

Then I remembered how, after the fire, he'd chased me with his riding crop. His face hardened into the same angry mask he'd worn that day.

He let go of the whip and rubbed his palms against the side of his coat. "I've been too soft on you," he said under his breath, and turned his back on me.

Mother stood in front of a small medieval stretching rack. The relic must've dated clear back to the Inquisition. She seemed alarmed to find such an evil contraption housed in a girls' school. But as she rubbed her fingertips together I realized she wasn't alarmed, merely perturbed that dust had smudged the tips of her glove.

I wanted to scream. *No, no, no!* People do not do this anymore. Not to their daughters. Not to anyone. And yet here we were, standing before implements of reform that even the despicable Miss Stranje had not invented; whips, paddles, various length training rods, and other devices, like the backboard that were in use all over England.

I swallowed the pincushion of fear stuck in my throat and, marshaled every ounce of courage I had left, to ask, "You don't actually use this rack, do you?"

Miss Stranje turned to me, hideously pleasant, as if merely commenting on the weather. "I find it remarkably effective."

Father headed for the door. "I've seen enough. I'm ready to sign those damnable papers of yours. I want to be rid of this place."

Rid of me.

Mother and Miss Stranje hurried after him. I stared at the shackles on the rack, stunned that my parents would leave me at the mercy of this awful school. I'm not given to outbursts of weakness, but I began to tremble stupidly and my feet seemed frozen to the cold stone floor.

Hope does not shatter all at once. The mind plays tricks.

For several moments I felt certain Stranje House was no more than a ghoulish nightmare. Any moment, I assured myself, my maid Agnes would throw back the curtains and I would awaken in my own bedroom. The world would turn right again. Sanity would return. The sun would glint through my windows. The mantel clock would tick steadily and reliably, not like the panicky thumping of my heart.

But I did not wake up. Not until Madame Cho swatted the back of my legs with her stick and pointed to the door. "You go." Then she turned and beat on the mummy case. My stinging calves roused me out of disbelief.

I ran.

My slippers skidded against the stone floor as I dashed out of that ghastly room. Faint candlelight trickled from the discipline chamber, but not nearly enough to penetrate the thick darkness in the hallway. Still I ran. Straining to see my way through the inky blackness. A junction in the corridor confused me. Which way were the stairs? Behind me, Madame Cho's banging mingled with yelps of pain. I shook my head. This wasn't a girls' school. It was a madhouse.

I had no idea what Napoleon intended to do about his imprisonment on Elba, but as for me, I planned to escape.

A SCHOOL FOR UNUSUAL GIRLS,
A Stranje House Novel

Print and eBook are available at all fine booksellers.

Barnes & Noble

Amazon

Powells

iBooks

Indiebound

BooksaMillion

Ebooks.com

Googleplay

Also available online is
Kathleen's Humorous Traditional Regency
Romance Series, *My Notorious Aunt*

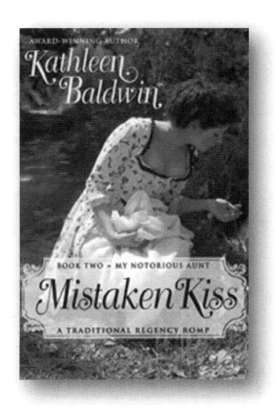

Mistaken Kiss

Book 2, My Notorious Aunt
A Traditional Regency Romantic Romp

Willa is nearly blind, but she recognizes trouble when she trips over it.

THE VICAR'S LOGICAL little sister knows her prospects are bleak. When Willa accidentally kisses Alexander Braeburn, her dull predictable world turns upside down. Reason dictates that she should stay away from the handsome Corinthian. He's the black sheep of their village. But how can she resist? She longs for one more taste of the most tantalizing excitement she has ever experienced. One more marvelous kiss, that's all she wants, and then she will settle back into her dreary life forever.

Alex is intrigued. Willa's refreshingly genuine character warms his jaded heart and makes him smile. But when her notorious aunt whisks her off to London and Willa naïvely marches into trouble, Alex feels duty bound to rescue her. Is it duty? Or is something else compelling him to watch over the vicar's peculiar little sister?

Excerpt available at Barnes & Noble, Amazon, or KathleenBaldwin.com

OTHER BOOKS BY KATHLEEN BALDWIN

———— ✂ ————

MY NOTORIOUS AUNT SERIES

HUMOROUS TRADITIONAL REGENCY NOVELS

LADY FIASCO

MISTAKEN KISS

CUT FROM THE SAME CLOTH

———— ✂ ————

FROM TORTEEN (MACMILLAN)

EXCITING NEW REGENCY ROMANCE YA SERIES

THE STRANJE HOUSE NOVELS

A SCHOOL FOR UNUSUAL GIRLS

EXILE FOR DREAMERS

REFUGE FOR MASTERMINDS

———— ✂ ————

CONTEMPORARY TEEN FANTASY

DIARY OF A TEENAGE FAIRY GODMOTHER